"But you do want to find a solution, right?" Aristotle lounged back, his arm resting easily against the side of the chair, and suddenly Teddie wanted to reach out and touch the golden skin, run her fingertips over the smooth curve of muscle pressing against the fabric of his shirt.

"What? Yes—yes, of course I do." She dragged her eyes away, up to the compelling dark eyes and dangerous curves of his face.

He nodded. "Something stable and uncomplicated, I think you said."

"Yes, that's what I want but--" She gazed at him uncertainly, wondering exactly where the conversation was going.

"Then the solution is staring us in the face." He went on as if she hadn't spoken, his voice curling over her skin, soothing and unsettling her at the same time.

"What do you mean?" she said hoarsely.

He smiled. "Isn't it obvious? We need to get married."

Secret Heirs of Billionaires

There are some things money can't buy...

Living life at lightning pace, these magnates are no strangers to stakes at their highest. It seems they've got it all... That is, until they find out that there's an unplanned item to add to their list of accomplishments!

Achieved:

1. Successful business empire.

2. Beautiful women in their bed.

3. *An heir to bear their name?*

Though every billionaire needs to leave his legacy in safe hands, discovering a secret heir shakes up the carefully orchestrated plan in more ways than one!

Uncover their secrets in:

Wed for His Secret Heir by Chantelle Shaw

The Heir the Prince Secures by Jennie Lucas

The Italian's Unexpected Love-Child by Miranda Lee

The Baby the Billionaire Demands by Jennie Lucas

Married for His One-Night Heir by Jennifer Hayward

The Secret Kept from the Italian by Kate Hewitt

Look out for more stories in the
Secret Heirs of Billionaires series coming soon!

Louise Fuller

DEMANDING HIS SECRET SON

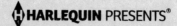

Recycling programs
for this product may
not exist in your area.

ISBN-13: 978-1-335-53804-8

Demanding His Secret Son

First North American publication 2019

Copyright © 2019 by Louise Fuller

Printed in U.S.A.

Louise Fuller was a tomboy who hated pink and always wanted to be the prince—not the princess! Now she enjoys creating heroines who aren't pretty pushovers but are strong, believable women. Before writing for Harlequin she studied literature and philosophy at university, and then worked as a reporter on her local newspaper. She lives in Tunbridge Wells with her impossibly handsome husband, Patrick, and their six children.

Books by Louise Fuller

Harlequin Presents

Vows Made in Secret
A Deal Sealed by Passion
Claiming His Wedding Night
Blackmailed Down the Aisle
Kidnapped for the Tycoon's Baby
Surrender to the Ruthless Billionaire
Revenge at the Altar

Visit the Author Profile page
at Harlequin.com for more titles.

For Archie: for sticking at the hard stuff, and making life easier for everyone around you, especially me.

Louise x

CHAPTER ONE

LEANING FORWARD, TEDDIE TAYLOR spread the three playing cards out swiftly, then quickly flipped them over, covering them with her hand and rearranging them. Her green eyes gave away none of her excitement, nor the jump of her heart as the man sitting opposite her pointed confidently at the middle card.

He groaned as she turned it over, holding his hands up in defeat. 'Incredible,' he murmured.

Rising to his feet, Edward Claiborne held out his hand, a satisfied smile creasing his smooth patrician features.

'I can't tell you how happy I am that you're on board.' His blue eyes fixed on Teddie's face. 'I'm looking forward to having a little magic in my life.'

Teddie smiled. From another, younger, less urbane man, the remark might have sounded a little cheesy. But she knew Claiborne was far too well-bred to do anything as crass and inappropriate as flirt with a woman half his age to whom he had just given a job at his new prestigious private members' club.

'I'm looking forward to it too, Mr Claiborne— no, please—' she stopped him as he reached into the pocket of his jacket '—let me get these.' She gestured towards the coffee. 'You're a client now.'

Watching him walk away to talk to someone in the hotel lounge, she took a deep breath and sat down, resisting the urge to pump the air with her fist in time to the victory chant inside her head. She'd done it! Finally she'd netted a client who saw magic as more than just an amusing diversion at a party.

Across the lounge, Edward Claiborne was shaking hands, smiling smoothly and, leaning back in her armchair, she let elation wash over her. This was what she and Elliot had been chasing, but this new contract was worth more to them than a paycheque. Claiborne was fifth generation New York money and a recommendation from him would give their business the kind of publicity they couldn't buy.

Pulling out her phone, she punched in Elliot's number. He answered immediately, almost as though he'd been waiting for her to call—which, of course, he had.

'That was quick. How did it go?'

He sounded as he always did, speaking with that casual west-coast drawl that people sometimes mistook for slowness or lack of comprehension. But to Teddie, who had known him since she was thirteen, there was a tension to his voice—understandably. A three-nights-a-week job of bringing magic and illusion to the brand-new Castine Club would not only boost their income, it would mean they could employ someone to do the day-to-day admin. And that would mean they wouldn't end up with a repeat of today's last-minute panic when Elliot had realised he'd double-booked himself.

For a moment, she considered making him sweat, but she was too happy and relieved. 'He's in!'

Hearing Elliot's triumphant 'Surf's up, baby!' she laughed.

It was one of the things she loved most about her business partner and best friend—the way he reverted to his Californian roots when he was excited. Her heart swelled. That and the fact that, no matter how unjustified it was, he always had complete faith in her.

'I'm not saying I thought it was guaranteed, but honestly—I don't think I've ever met anyone who loves magic so much.'

'So what clinched it? No, let me guess. The three-card Monte. I'm right, aren't I?'

Teddie could practically picture the familiar wicked grin on Elliot's face.

'Yes! But that doesn't mean I forgive you for throwing me in at the deep end.'

He laughed. 'So how about I take you and George to Pete's Grill at the weekend? To make amends and celebrate?'

'You're on.' She frowned. 'How come you're talking to me, anyway? I thought the whole reason I had to do this was because you had a meeting.'

'I do—I'm waiting to go in. Actually, I'm going to have to go—okay, babe? But I'll drop round later.' He whooped. 'I love this job!'

He hung up, and Teddie grinned. She loved her job too, and Elliot was right: they should celebrate. And George loved Pete's.

Thinking about her son, Teddie felt her heart tighten. She did love her job, but her love for George was fierce and absolute. From the moment she'd held him in her arms after his birth, her heart had been enslaved by his huge dark eyes.

He was perfect, and he was hers. And maybe, if this job went well, in a couple of years they'd be celebrating here.

Leaning back against the smooth leather upholstery of a chair that probably cost more than her car, Teddie glanced around the hotel lounge. Well, maybe not here. The Kildare Hotel was new, and completely beyond her pay grade, oozing a mixture of old-school comfort and avant-garde design that she might have found intimidating if she hadn't been feeling so euphoric.

It was clearly the place to be seen, judging by the mix of hip, moneyed guests, although—she stared critically at the two huge Warhol prints that dwarfed one wall—wasn't it a bit corny to have all these copies of famous paintings hanging everywhere. Why not use originals by local artists?

Glancing over to where Claiborne was still chatting, she felt her pulse skitter forward. Really, she should be over there too, networking. It didn't have to be too obvious. All she had to do was smile as she passed by and her new boss would definitely call her over to introduce her to his companion.

She couldn't see the man's face, but even at a distance his glamour and self-assurance were tangible. Silhouetted against the industrial-sized window, with sunlight fanning around him like a sunburst, he looked almost mythical. The effect was mesmerising, irresistible—and, catching sight of the furtive glances of the other guests, she realised that it wasn't only she who thought so.

She wondered idly if he was aware of the effect he was having or if he was worthy of all the attention. Maybe she should just go and see for herself, she thought, emboldened by her business triumph.

And then, as she began picking up the cards that were still strewn all over the table, she noticed that Claiborne was gesturing in her direction. Automatically her lips started to curve upwards as the man standing beside him turned towards her.

The welcoming smile froze on her face.

She swallowed thickly. Her heart felt hard and heavy—in fact, her whole body seemed to be slowly turning to stone. Her euphoria of just moments earlier felt like a muddied memory.

No—no way! This couldn't be happening. He couldn't be here. Not here, not now.

But he was. Worse, having shaken hands with Claiborne, he was excusing himself and walking— no, *swaggering* towards her, his familiar dark gaze locked with hers. And, despite the alarm shrieking inside her head, she couldn't drag her eyes away from his cold, staggeringly handsome face and lean, muscular body.

For just a split second she watched him make his way across the room, and then her heart began pounding like a jackhammer and she knew that she had to move, to run, to flee. It might not be dignified, but frankly she didn't care. Her ex-husband, Aristotle Leonidas, was the last person on earth she wanted to see, much less talk to. There was too much history between them—not just a failed marriage, but a three-year-old son he knew nothing about.

Snatching at the rest of the cards, she tried to force them into the box. Only, panic made her clumsier than usual and they slipped out of her hands, spilling onto the floor in every direction.

'Allow me.'

If it had been a shock seeing him across the room, seeing him up close was like being struck by lightning. It would have been easier if he'd developed a paunch, but he hadn't changed at all. If anything, he was more devastating than ever, and it was clear that he had risen to such a point of power and wealth that he was immune to such earthly concerns as appearances.

But, to Teddie, his beauty was still hypnotic—the knife-sharp bone structure and obsidian-dark eyes still too perfect to be human.

Feeling her pulse accelerate, Teddie steeled herself to meet his gaze.

It had been four years since he'd broken her heart and turned his back on the gift of her love, but she had never forgotten him nor forgiven him for deleting her—and by default George—from his life like some unsolicited junk email. But evidently she had underestimated the impact of his husky, seductive voice—or why else was her pulse shying sideways like a startled pony?

It was just shock, she reassured herself. After four years she was obviously not expecting to see him.

Pushing aside the memory of that moment when he'd dismissed her like some underperforming junior member of his staff, she frowned. 'I'm fine. Just leave it.'

He ignored her, crouching down and calmly and methodically picking up each and every card.

'Here.' Standing up, he held out the pack, but

she stared at him tensely, reluctant to risk even the slightest physical contact between them.

Her body's irrational response to hearing him speak again had made her realise that despite everything he'd done—and not done—there was still a connection between them, a memory of what had once been, how good it had been—

Ignoring both that unsettling thought, and the tug of his gaze, she sat down. She wanted to leave, but she would have to push past him to do so, and sitting seemed like the lesser of two evils. He watched her for a moment, as though gauging the likelihood of her trying to escape, and then she felt her pulse jolt forward as he settled into the chair recently vacated by Claiborne.

'What are you doing here?' she said stiffly.

After they'd split up he'd moved to London—or that was what Elliot had been told when he'd gone to collect her things. The apartment hadn't been part of the divorce settlement, and she'd always assumed he'd sold it. But then, he had no need of money, and it probably had no bad memories for him as he'd hardly ever been there.

His level gaze swept over her face. 'In New York?' He shrugged. 'I'm living here. Again,' he added softly.

She swallowed, stung at the thought of him returning to their home and simply picking up where he'd left off. She wished she could think of something devastating to say back to him. But to do so would only suggest that she cared—which she obviously didn't.

She watched warily as he slid the pack across the table towards her.

Catching sight of her expression, he tutted under his breath, his dark brown eyes narrowing. 'I don't know why you're looking at me like that,' he said coolly. 'It's me who should be worried. Or at least checking my wrist.'

His gaze hovered on her face and she blinked. She'd thought her body's unintended and unwelcome response to his was a by-product of shock, but now, beneath the politeness, further down than the hostility, she could feel it still—a thread of heat that was undiminished by time or reason. It made no sense—she doubted that he'd given her as much as a passing thought in the last four years—but that didn't seem to stop her skin from tingling beneath his gaze.

Watching the fury flare in her fabulous green eyes, Aristo gritted his teeth. She was still as stubborn as ever, but he was grateful she hadn't taken the cards from him. If both his hands had been free he might have been tempted to strangle her.

He hadn't spotted Teddie when he'd first walked into the lounge, partly because her dark brown hair was not falling loosely to her shoulders, as it had done when he'd last seen her, but was folded neatly at the back of her head.

In the main, though, he hadn't spotted her because, frankly, he hadn't ever expected to see his ex-wife again. He felt a tiny stab of pain in his heart like a splinter of ice.

But then, why would he?

Four years ago Theodora Taylor had ensnared him with her green eyes, her long legs and her diffident manner. She had breezed into his life like the Sirocco, interrupting his calm and ordered ascent into the financial stratosphere, and then just as quickly she had gone, an emptied bank account and his lacerated heart the only reminders of their six-month marriage.

He gave her a long, implacable stare. Teddie had taken more than his money. She had stolen the beat from his heart and taken what little trust he'd had for women and trampled it into the ground. It had been the first time he'd let down his guard, even going so far as to honour her with his name, but she had only married him in the hope that his money and connections would act as a stepping stone to a better life.

Of course he hadn't realised the truth until he'd returned from a business trip to find her gone. Hurt and humiliated, he had thrown himself into his job and put the whole disastrous episode behind him.

Until he'd bumped into Edward Claiborne a moment ago. He knew Edward socially, and liked him for his quiet self-assurance and old-school courtesy.

Walking into the hotel lounge, he'd noticed him laughing and chatting with uncharacteristic animation to a female companion. But it had only been when Edward had invited him to the new regular magic slot at his club, and then mentioned that he'd just finished having coffee with the woman who'd be running the shows, that he had turned and seen Teddie.

The muscle in his jaw had flexed, kick-starting a chain reaction through his body so that suddenly his heart had been pounding so hard and fast that he'd felt almost dizzy.

He studied her silently now, safe in the knowledge that his external composure gave no hint of the battle raging inside him. His head was telling him there was only one course of action. That a sensible, sane man would get up and walk away. But sense and sanity had never played that much of a part in his relationship with Theodora Taylor, and clearly nothing had changed—because despite knowing that she was the biggest mistake he had ever made, he stayed sitting.

His lip curled as he glanced down at his wrist. 'No, still there. But maybe I should double-check my wallet. Or perhaps I should give Edward Claiborne a call...make sure he still has his. I know you were only having coffee, but you were always a quick worker. I should know.'

Teddie felt her cheeks grow warm. His face was impenetrable, but the derision in his voice as much as his words was insultingly obvious.

How dare he talk to her like that? As though she was the bad guy when he was the one who had cut her out of his life without so much as a word.

Not that she'd ever been high on his list of priorities. Six months of married life had made it clear that Aristo had no time in his life for a wife. Even when she'd moved out and they'd begun divorce proceedings, he'd carried on working as though nothing had happened. Although no amount of his neglect and indifference could have prepared her for how he'd behaved at the end.

It had been a mistake, sleeping together that last time.

With emotions running high after a meeting to discuss their divorce, they'd ended up in bed and she'd ended up pregnant. Only, by the time she'd realised that her tiredness and nausea weren't just symptoms of stress, the divorce had been finalised, and Aristo had been on the other side of the world, building his European operations.

Although he might just as well have been in outer space.

Remembering her repeated, increasingly desperate and unsuccessful attempts to get in touch, she felt her back stiffen. She'd been frantic to tell him she was pregnant, but his complete radio silence had made it clear—horribly, humiliatingly clear—not only that he didn't want to talk to her, but that he didn't want to listen to *anything* she had to say.

It had been during a call to his London office, when an over-officious PA had cut short her stumbling and not very coherent attempt to speak to him, that she had decided doing the right thing was not going to work.

It certainly hadn't worked for her parents.

Sometimes it was better to face the truth, even if it was painful—and, truthfully, she and Aristo's relationship had had pretty flimsy foundations. Judging by the mess they'd made of their marriage, it certainly wasn't strong enough to cope with an unplanned pregnancy.

But it had been hard.

Aristo's rejection had broken her heart, and the repercussions of their brief and ill-fated marriage had lasted longer than her tears. Even now, she was still so wary of men that she'd barely gone out with anyone since they'd parted ways. Thanks to her father's casual, cursory attitude to parenting, she found it hard to believe that she would ever be anything more than an afterthought to any man. Aristo's casual, cruel rejection had confirmed that deep-seated privately held fear.

Much as she cared for Elliot, it was as a sister.

Aristo was still the only man she'd ever loved. He had been her first love—not her first lover, but he had taught her everything about pleasure.

Her green eyes lifted to his. And not just pleasure. Because of him she'd become an authority on heartache and regret too.

So what exactly gave *him* the right to stand there with a sneer on that irritatingly handsome face?

Suddenly she was glad she hadn't turned tail. Fingers curling into fists, she glared at him. 'I think your memory must be playing tricks on you, Aristo. Work was always your thing—not mine. And, not that it's any of your concern, but Edward Claiborne is a very generous man. He was more than happy to pay the bill.'

She knew how she was making it sound, but it wasn't quite a lie. He *had* offered to pay. And besides, if it made Aristo feel even a fraction of her pain, then why not rub it in? He might not have thought her worthy of his attention and commitment, but Edward had been happy to give her his time and his company.

'And that's what matters to you, isn't it, Theodora? Getting your bills paid. Even if it means taking what isn't yours.'

He didn't really care about the money—even before his ruthless onwards-and-upwards rise to global domination, the amount she'd taken had been a negligible amount. Now it would barely make a dent in the Leonidas billions. At the time, though, it had stung—particularly as it had been down to his own stupidity.

For some unknown reason he hadn't closed their shared accounts immediately after the divorce was finalised, and Teddie had wasted no time taking advantage. Not that he should have been surprised. No matter how pampered they were, women were never satisfied with what they had. He'd learned that aged six, when his mother had found a titled, wealthier replacement for his father.

But knowing Teddie had worked her 'magic' on Edward hurt—and, childish though it was, he wanted to hurt her back.

Her eyes narrowed. 'It was mine,' she said hotly. '*It was ours.* That's what marriage is about, Aristo— it's called sharing.'

He stared at her disparagingly. The briefness of their marriage and the ruthless determination of his legal team had ensured that her financial settlement had been minimal, but it was more than she deserved.

'Is that what you tell yourself?'

She felt the hairs stand up on the back of her neck as he shook his head slowly.

'Just because it was still a joint account that didn't mean you had the right to empty it.'

'If it bothered you that much you could have

talked to me,' she snarled. 'But I was only your wife—why would you want to talk to me?'

'Don't give me that,' he said sharply. 'I talked to you.'

'You talked at me about work. Never about us.'

Never about the fact that they were basically living separate lives—two strangers sharing a bed but never a meal or a joke.

Hearing the emotion in her voice, she stopped abruptly. What was the point of having this conversation? It was four years too late, and their marriage couldn't have mattered that much to him if all he wanted to discuss now was their bank account.

And was it really that surprising? His whole life had been dedicated to making money.

She breathed in unsteadily. 'And, as for the money, I took what I needed to live.'

To look after our son, she thought with a sudden flare of anger. A son who even before his birth had been relegated to second place.

'I'm not going to apologise for that, and if it was a problem then you should have said something at the time, but you made it quite clear that you didn't want to talk to me.'

Aristo stared at her, anger pulsing beneath his skin. At the time he had seen her behaviour as just more evidence of his poor judgement. More proof that the women in his life would inevitably turn their backs on him.

But he was not about to reveal his reasons for staying silent—why should he? He wasn't the one who'd walked out on their marriage. He didn't need to explain himself.

His heart began to thump rhythmically inside his chest, and an old, familiar feeling of bitter, impotent fury formed a knot in his stomach. She was right. He should have dealt with this years ago—because even though he had succeeded in erasing her from his heart and his home, he had never quite managed to wipe her betrayal from his memory.

How could he, though? Their relationship had been over so quickly and had ended with such finality that there had been no time to confront her properly.

Until now.

Teddie stared at him in appalled silence as, leaning back, he stretched out his legs. Moments earlier she had wanted to throw George's existence in his face. Now, though, she could feel spidery panic scuttling over her skin at the thought of how close she'd come to revealing the truth.

'So let's talk now,' he said, turning to nod curtly at a passing waiter, who hurried over with almost comical haste.

She nearly laughed, only it was more sad than funny. He didn't want to talk now any more than he had four years ago, but he knew that she wanted to leave so he wanted to make her stay. Nothing had changed. He hadn't changed. He just wanted to get his own way.

'An espresso, please, and an Americano.' He gave the order without so much as looking at her, and the fact that he could still remember her favourite drink, as much as his arrogant assumption that she would be joining him, made her want to scream.

'I'm not staying,' she said coldly. She knew from past experience that his powers of persuasion were incomparable, but in the past she had loved him to distraction. Here, in the present, she wasn't going to let him push her into a corner. 'And I don't want to speak to you,' she said, glancing pointedly past him.

He shrugged, a mocking smile curving his mouth. 'Then I'll talk and you can listen.'

Cheeks darkening with angry colour, she sat mutinously as the waiter reappeared and, with a swift, nervous glance at Aristo, deposited the drinks in front of them.

'Is there anything else, Mr Leonidas?'

Aristo shook his head. 'No, thank you.'

Teddie stared at him, a beat of irritation jumping in her chest. It was always the same, this effect that Aristo had on people. When they'd first met she'd teased him about it: as a magician, *she* was supposed to be the centre of attention. But even when his wealth had been visible but not daunting, he'd had something that set him apart from all the other beautiful rich people—a potent mix of power and beauty and vitality that created an irresistible gravitational pull around him.

She could hardly blame the poor waiter for being like a cat on hot bricks when she had been just as susceptible. It was still maddening, though.

Some of her feelings must be showing on her face, for as he reached to pick up his cup, he paused. 'Is there a problem?'

She raised her eyebrows. 'Other than you, you mean?'

He sighed. 'I meant with your drink. I can send it back.'

'Could you just stop throwing your weight around?' She shook her head in exasperation. 'I know it must be difficult for you to switch off from work, but this isn't one of your hotels.'

Leaning back, he raised the cup to his mouth, his eyes never leaving her face. 'Actually it is,' he said mildly. 'It's the first in a new line we're trying out—traditional elegance and luxury with impeccable sustainability.' He smiled at the look of frozen horror on her face. 'And a constantly rotating collection of contemporary art.'

She felt her breathing jerk as out of the corner of her eye she noticed the tiny lion's head logo on the coaster. Cheeks burning, she glanced furtively over at the Warhols.

Damn it, but of course they were real. Aristo Leonidas would never have anything in his life that wasn't one hundred per cent perfect—it was why he'd found it so devastatingly easy to abandon her.

Her heartbeat stumbled in her chest. No doubt he'd only wanted her to stay here so he could point out this latest addition to his empire.

Cursing herself, and Aristo, and Elliot for being so useless at managing their schedule, she half rose.

'Sit down,' he said softly.

Their eyes clashed. 'I don't want to.'

'Why? Are you scared of what will happen if you do?

Was she scared?

She felt her insides flip over, and she suddenly felt hot and dizzy.

Once she had been in thrall to him. He'd been everything she'd wanted in a lover and in a man. Caught in the dark shimmering intensity of his gaze, she had felt warm and wanted.

And now, as the heat spread outwards, she was forced to accept again that, even hating him as she did, her body was still reacting in the same way, unconstrained by logic or even the most basic sense of self-preservation.

Horrified by this revelation of her continuing vulnerability—or maybe stupidity—she lifted her chin, her eyes narrowing, muscles tensing as though for combat.

'I'm not, no. But *you* should be. Or maybe you like your suits with coffee stains?'

His dark eyes flickered with amusement. 'If you want me to get undressed, you could just ask.'

He was unbelievable and unfair, making such a blatant reference to their sexual past. But, despite her outrage, she felt the kick of desire. Just as she had that night four years ago, when her body had betrayed her.

Her heart thudded. How could she have let it happen? Just hours earlier they'd been thrashing out their divorce. She'd known he didn't love her, and yet she'd still slept with him.

But she could never fully regret her stupidity for that was the night she'd conceived George.

She glowered at him. 'I don't want you at all,' she lied. 'And I don't want to have some stupid conversation about coffee or art.'

He held up his hands in mock surrender. 'Okay, okay. Look, this is hard for both us, but we share a history. Surely if fate has chosen to throw us together we can put our differences behind us for old times' sake,' he said smoothly. 'Surely you can spare a couple of minutes to catch up.'

Teddie felt her heart start to pound. If only if was just the past they shared. But it wasn't, and hiding that fact from Aristo was proving harder than she'd ever imagined.

But how could she tell him the truth? That he

had a three-year-old son called George he'd never met. She caught her breath, trying to imagine how that conversation would start, much less end.

More importantly, though, why would she tell him? Their marriage might have been short-lived, but it had been long enough for her to know that there was no room in her ex-husband's life for anything but his career. And, having been on the receiving end of her father's intermittent attention, she knew exactly what it felt like to be a side dish to the main meal, and she was not about to let her son suffer the same fate.

'I just told you. I don't want to stay.' But, glancing up into his dark eyes, she felt a flare of panic, for they were cold and flat like slate, and they matched the uncompromising expression on his face.

'I wasn't actually giving you an option.'

She felt the colour leave her face. Had he really just said what she thought he had?

'What is that supposed to mean?' Instantly her panic was forgotten, obliterated in a white-out of fury. 'Just because this is your hotel, Aristo, it doesn't mean you can act like some despot,' she snapped.' If I want to leave, I will, thank you very much, and there's nothing you can do about it.'

Aristo stared at her in silence. Was this why he had sought out her company instead of simply retreating? To force a confrontation so that, unlike in their marriage, he would be the one to dictate when she left? Would that heal the still festering wound of her betrayal? Quiet the suspicion, the knowledge, that he had been used like a plaything to pass the time until something, or more likely *someone*, better came along?

He shrugged dismissively. 'That would depend, I suppose, on how you leave and whether you value your reputation. Being removed by Security in front of a room full of people could be quite damaging.' Leaning back in his seat, he raised an eyebrow. 'I can't imagine what your new boss would think if he heard about it.'

'You wouldn't dare,' she said softly.

His eyes didn't leave her face. 'Try me!'

He could see the conflict in her eyes—frustration and resentment battling with logic and resignation—but he knew the battle was already won. If she was going to leave she would already be on her feet.

With immense satisfaction he watched her sit back stiffly in her seat. This wasn't about revenge, but even so he couldn't help letting a small, triumphant smile curve his mouth.

'So…' He gestured towards the pack of cards. 'You're still a magician, then.'

Teddie stared at the cards. To anyone else his remark would have sounded innocuous, nothing more than a polite show of interest in an ex's current means of employment. But she wasn't anyone. She had been his wife, and she could hear the resentment in his voice for she had heard it before.

It was another reminder of why their marriage had failed. And why she should have confronted the past head-on instead of pretending her marriage had never happened. She might have been strong for her son, but she'd been a coward when it came to facing Aristo.

Only, she'd had good reason not to want to face him. Lots of good reasons, actually.

In the aftermath of their marriage he'd been cold and unapproachable, and later she'd been so sick with her pregnancy, and then, by the time she'd felt well again, George had been born—and that was a whole other conversation.

She was suddenly conscious of Aristo's steady, dark gaze and her heart gave a thump. She had to stop thinking about George or something was going to slip out.

'Yes,' she said curtly. 'I'm still a magician, Aristo. And you're still in hotels.'

Her heart was thumping hard against her chest. Did he really want to sit here with her while they politely pretended to be on speaking terms? Her hands felt suddenly damp and she pressed them against the cooling leather. Clearly he did. But then, he didn't have a secret to keep.

He nodded. 'Mostly, but I've diversified my interests.'

She gritted her teeth. So even less time for anything other than work. For some reason that thought made her feel sad rather than angry and, caught off-guard, she picked up her coffee and took a sip.

Aristo looked at her, his gaze impassive. 'You must have done well. Edward Claiborne doesn't often go out of his comfort zone. So how did you two meet?'

His eyes tangled with hers and he felt a stab of anger, remembering Edward Claiborne's proprietorial manner as he'd turned and gestured across the room towards Teddie.

She shrugged. 'Elliot and I did some magic showcases at a couple of charity balls last year and he was there.'

Aristo stared at her coldly. 'You work with Elliot?'

For some reason her defiant nod made a primitive jealousy rip through him like a box-cutter. In his head—if he'd allowed himself to picture her at all—she had been alone, suffering as he was. Only, now it appeared that not only had she survived, she was prospering with Elliot.

'We set up a business together. He does the admin, front of house and accountancy. I do the magic.'

He felt another spasm of irritation—pain, almost. He knew Teddie had never been romantically or sexually involved with Elliot, but he had supported her, and once that had been *his* job. It was bad enough that his half-brother, Oliver, had displaced him in his mother's affections—now it appeared that Elliot had usurped him in Teddie's.

'From memory, he wasn't much of a businessman,' he said coolly.

For the first time since she'd sat down Teddie smiled and, watching her eyes soften, he had to fight an overwhelming urge to reach out and stroke her cheek, for once her eyes had used to soften for him in that way.

'He's not, but he's my best friend and I trust him,' she said simply. 'And that's what matters.'

It was tempting to lie, to tell him that she'd found love and unimaginable passion in Elliot's arms, but it would only end up making her look sad and desperate.

He raised an eyebrow. 'Surely what matters is profit?'

She'd always known he felt like that, but somehow his remark hurt more than it should, for it was the reason her son would grow up without a father.

Her fingers curled. 'Some things are more important than money, Aristo.'

'Not in business,' he said dismissively.

She glared at him, hating him and his stupid,

blinkered view of life, but hating herself more for still caring what he thought.

'But there's more to life than business. There's feelings and people—friends, family—'

She broke off, the emotion in her voice echoing inside her head. Glancing up, she found him watching her, his gaze darkly impassive, and it was hard not to turn away, for the heartbreakingly familiar masculine beauty of his face seemed so at odds with the distance in his eyes.

'You don't have a family,' he said.

It was one of the few facts she'd shared with him about her life—that she was an orphan. Dazed, Teddie blinked. She was about to retort that she was a mother to his son, when abruptly her brain came back online and she bit back her words. Given how he'd behaved, and was still behaving, she certainly didn't owe him the truth.

But George was his child. Didn't he deserve to know that?

Her heartbeat stalled, and for a moment she couldn't breathe. Her stomach seemed to be turning in on itself. Wishing that she could make herself disappear as effortlessly as she could make watches and wallets vanish, she forced herself to meet his gaze.

'No, I don't,' she lied.

And suddenly she knew that she had to leave right there and then, for to stay would mean more lies, and she couldn't do it—she didn't want to lie about her son.

Neither could she carry on lying to herself.

Up until today she had wanted to believe that she was over Aristo. But as she stared into his dark, distant eyes, the pain of pretending erupted inside of her, and suddenly she needed to make certain this *never* happened again.

She'd made the mistake of letting him back into her life before—made the mistake of following her heart, not her head. And although she didn't regret it—for that would mean regretting having her son—after that one-night stand she'd accepted not only that their marriage was over, but that it was the best possible outcome.

Only by staying out of his orbit would she be safe—not just from him, but from herself.

She lifted her chin. This meeting would be their last.

Ignoring the intensity of his dark gaze, and the full, sensuous mouth that had so often kissed her into a state of helpless bliss, she cleared her throat. 'Fascinating though this is, Aristo, I don't really think there's any point in us carrying on with this conversation,' she said. 'Small talk—any kind of talk, really—wasn't ever your strong point, and we got divorced for a reason—several, actually.'

He held her gaze. 'Are you refusing to talk to me?'

'Yes, I am.'

But she didn't want to explain why. Didn't want to explain the complex and conflicting emotions swirling inside her.

Her heart was banging against her ribs and, breathing in deeply, she steadied herself. Reaching into her bag, she pulled out a pen and a notebook and scrawled something on a page inside it. Tearing the page free, she folded it in half and slid it onto the table.

'I don't expect to hear from you again, but if you have to get in touch this is my lawyer's number. Goodbye, Aristotle.'

And then, before he'd even had a chance to react, let alone respond, she turned and almost ran out of the hotel lounge.

Left alone, Aristo stared at the empty seat, a mass of emotions churning inside him. His heart was beating out of time. Teddie's words had shocked him. But, although she had no doubt intended her curt goodbye to be a slap in the face, to him it felt as though she'd thrown down a gauntlet at his feet.

And in doing so she'd sealed her fate. Four years ago she had waltzed out of their marriage and his life and he'd spent the intervening years suppressing hurt and disappointment. Now, though, he was ready to confront his past—*and* his ex-wife.

But he would do so on his terms, he thought coldly. And, reaching into his jacket, he pulled out his phone.

* * *

Three hours later, having fed and bathed George and tidied away his toys, Teddie leaned back against the faded cushions of her sofa and let out a long, slow breath. She felt exhausted. Her apartment—her wonderful apartment—with its bright walls and wooden floors, which was usually a place of sanctuary, looked shabby after the high gloss of the Kildare Hotel. And, although her son was usually a sweet-tempered and easy-going toddler, he must have picked up on her tension. Tonight he'd had a huge tantrum when she'd stopped him playing with his toy speed boat in the bath.

He was sleeping now, and as she'd gazed down at her beautiful son she had felt both pride and panic, for he so resembled his father. A father he would never know.

She felt a rush of guilt and self-pity. This wasn't what she'd wanted for herself or for her son. In her dreams she'd wanted to give him everything she'd never had—two loving parents, financial security—but she'd tried marriage and it had been a disaster.

Even before Aristo's obsession with work had blotted out the rest of his life she had felt like a gatecrasher in her own marriage. But then what had they really known about one another? How could you really know someone after just seven weeks? Maybe if their marriage had had stronger foundations it might have been possible for them to face their problems together. But they'd had no common ground aside from a raging sexual attraction which had been enough to blind both of them to their fundamental incompatibility. He had been born into wealth. She, on the other hand, had grown up in a children's home with a mother dosed up on prescription drugs and a father in prison.

And sex wasn't enough to sustain a relationship—not without trust and openness and tenderness.

Divorce had been the only option, and, although she might be able to face that fact she still wasn't up to facing Aristo. Thankfully, though, she would never have to see him again.

Her pulse twitched as she remembered telling him to talk to her through her lawyer. She could hardly believe that she'd spoken to him like that. But she'd been so desperate to leave before she said anything incriminating about George, and even more desperate to ensure that he would be out of her life for good.

Stifling a yawn, she picked up her phone and gazed gloomily down at the time on the screen. All she wanted to do was crawl into bed, pull the duvet over her head and forget about the mess she'd made of her life.

Unfortunately Elliot was dropping round to discuss the Claiborne meeting.

For a moment she considered calling him to cancel. But being on her own with a head full of regrets and recriminations was not a great idea.

Anticipating Elliot's partisan comments as she relayed an edited version of the day's events, she felt her mood lighten a fraction and, standing up, she walked into the tiny kitchen that led off from the living room.

She was just pulling a bottle of wine from the rack when she heard the entryphone.

Thank goodness! Elliot was early. Buzzing him up, she picked up a bottle of wine and two glasses.

'Don't be thinking we're going to finish this—' she began as she yanked open the door.

But her words trailed off into silence. It wasn't Elliot standing there, with that familiar affectionate grin on his face. Instead it was Aristo, and he wasn't smiling affectionately. In fact, he wasn't smiling at all.

CHAPTER TWO

'I WOULDN'T DREAM of it,' he said softly.

He held out his hand, his eyes locking with hers, and his sudden, swift smile made her heart lurch forward.

'You forgot these, and I was passing so...'

It was the pack of cards she'd left at his hotel.

She felt her breathing jerk. For a few seconds she couldn't answer—couldn't find the words to express her shock and confusion at finding him on her doorstep. Actually, not *on* her doorstep— he was already leaning against the frame, one foot resting negligently over the threshold so that shutting the door wouldn't just be a challenge, but a virtual impossibility, given the disparity in their respective weights.

'You were passing?'

She felt a shiver run over her skin as his dark gaze made a slow inspection of her, from the damp hair tumbling over her shoulders to her bare toes. Even if she'd been fully clothed she would have felt naked under his intense scrutiny, but she was wearing nothing but a T-shirt that was barely covered by her bathrobe.

There was a pulsing silence and then, tilting his head slightly, he glanced past her into the apartment. 'Aren't you going to invite me in? Or do you always entertain your guests in the corridor?'

'You're not a guest. Guests are invited, and I didn't invite you.' She stared at him suspiciously. 'And I didn't tell you where I lived either, so how did you find me?'

'I looked up "beautiful female magician" in the phone book.' His dark eyes glittered with amusement. 'You were there—right at the top.'

Her skin was suddenly prickling, her stomach flipping over in response to his words. She'd spent so long remembering his flaws that she had forgotten he could make her laugh and it was an untimely reminder of why she'd fallen in love with him.

Only, even as her mouth began to curl upwards she knew she was making a mistake. The last thing she needed right now was to give him any hint of her continuing vulnerability where he was concerned so, tuning out the erratic beat of her heart, she shook her head. 'Aristo—'

'Okay, that was a lie.' He shifted against the doorframe. 'I actually looked up "*angry*, beautiful female magician".'

Heart banging against her ribs, she took a deep breath, a rush of panic swamping her as she tried to gauge his mood. Surely if he'd found out about George he would be the angry one.

'Did you follow me?'

His smile widened. 'Of course. I have a second job as a private detective.'

Resisting the overriding urge to slam the door on his obviously expensive handmade shoes, she held his gaze. 'Very funny. So you had somebody find out where I lived?' She shook her head again. 'That's classy, Aristo.'

'You gave me no choice. You left before we'd finished talking.'

His complete inability to understand what had happened back at the hotel sucked her breath from her lungs.

'No, *I* had finished talking, Aristo,' she said irritably. 'That's why I gave you the number of my lawyer.'

'Ah, yes, your lawyer.' Pausing, he glanced over his shoulder and frowned, pretending concern. 'Are you sure you want everyone hearing about your private business?'

Teddie stared at him helplessly. She could tell from the glint in his eyes that he was not going to leave without saying whatever it was he wanted to say, and she couldn't physically remove him herself.

Maybe she should call for back-up. But who would she call? Her maintenance charge for the apartment included a caretaker who was nominally responsible for security, but she had no idea how to get in touch with him, and Aristo might make a scene and wake George.

So that left her with the choice of having a conversation in the hallway or in her apartment. Her heart contracted with apprehension. Every instinct she had was screeching at her like a banshee not to let him into her apartment, but what if he met one of her neighbours and they mentioned her son?

Maybe there were other options, but right now she was too tired and strung out to work them out—and besides, she wanted him out of the hallway and her life.

Quickly she did an inventory of the apartment—thankfully she had tidied George's toys away, and the only photos of him were in her bedroom. Her skin felt suddenly hot and tight, but of course there was no way Aristo would be going within a mile of that particular room.

'Fine. You can come in,' she said briskly. 'But you can't stay long.'

Mentally crossing her fingers, she hoped that to-night wouldn't be the one occasion when Elliot was on time. She had, of course, given him an abridged version of her ill-starred marriage, only she had carefully edited out all mention of the tangle of unresolved feelings she still carried around with her.

But Elliot would only have to walk through her front door to know that she was upset, and right now she had enough going on with Aristo. She certainly didn't want to have to deal with Elliot as well.

'Ten minutes, Aristo, that's all. And you'll have to be quiet. I have elderly neighbours,' she lied, 'and I don't want to disturb them.'

His dark, unwavering gaze fixed on hers and she felt a sudden rush of panic, for it seemed as though he could not only sense her lies, but also the reason behind them—as if the T-shirt she was wearing was printed with the truth.

'I can do quiet, Theodora. Or have you forgotten?'

Her pulse fluttered, cheeks suddenly burning. No, she hadn't forgotten. They had often been caught out by the strength of their desire, and on one particularly memorable occasion in a park they had satisfied their passion beneath the shade of a tree, hidden from passers-by. Quickly she pushed the thought away, wishing her brain hadn't chosen to save that particular memory for posterity, but not even divorce proceedings had weakened the devastating pull of desire between them.

Ignoring the quivering tension of her body, she lifted her chin and smiled at him coolly. 'It must have slipped my memory.'

Turning, she let the door fall back on his foot, his grunt of pain giving her a momentary but sharp satisfaction.

Stopping what she considered a safe distance

away from him, she watched as he strolled into her living room, his assessing gaze travelling over the modest interior and no doubt contrasting it with the luxury of the apartment they'd once shared. But who cared what he thought? He was only here under sufferance, and she needed to make that clear to him.

'I gave you my lawyer's number for a reason. So why are you here?' she asked stiffly.

She didn't much care, but now that he was standing in her living room she realised there was no such thing as *safe* for her where Aristo was concerned. He was still wearing his suit, but he'd unbuttoned his shirt and lost the tie. Only, instead of making him less intimidating, his more relaxed appearance only seemed to emphasise his natural authority.

Add to that the fact that they were completely alone, it was no surprise that her head was starting to swim.

But it wasn't just the tantalising temptation of his nearness that was making her hold her breath. Earlier she'd been so concerned about inadvertently revealing something about George that she'd been able to ignore her guilt at not doing so. In the unfamiliar surroundings of the Kildare Hotel it had felt almost like someone else's life.

Now, though, it felt real, *personal*, and she could feel herself wavering. Could she really go through with this? Could she really cheat him out of knowing his son? Shouldn't she at least give him the chance? And what about George? He'd already asked her why he didn't have a daddy.

So far he was too young to really focus on the issue, but that would change…

'I didn't speak to her.'

It took her a moment to realise that he was replying to her question about her lawyer.

He was standing with his back to her, studying the books on her shelves, and she stared tensely at him, remembering how he'd loved to lie with that same head on her lap and how she'd loved to run her fingers through the thick, black hair…

She jumped slightly as he turned, her cheeks flushing with colour as his all-seeing dark eyes fixed on hers.

'There was no point,' he said blithely. 'Why pay legal fees when we can talk for free?'

Her skin felt suddenly too tight. There was a long, steady silence as she stared at him incredulously. If she hadn't been so stunned, she might have laughed. 'Are you giving me advice?'

There was another long silence, and then he shrugged. 'Somebody has to. Clearly whoever has been doing so up until now can't have had your best interests at heart.'

He watched her green eyes widen, feeling childishly but intensely gratified that his words had clearly scored a direct hit. And then he caught sight of the two glasses and abruptly his mood changed, for clearly she hadn't been planning on spending the evening alone.

Ever since she'd more or less fled from him, he'd been questioning her motives for doing so. Although he knew their relationship was purely professional, Edward Claiborne and Teddie had looked good together, and it had got to him—for, just like his mother, Teddie was not the kind of women to be alone. Despite her denial, he had no doubt that somewhere in the city there was a nameless, faceless man who had stepped into his shoes.

In fact that was why he'd found himself standing on her doorstep. Even just imagining it made a knot of rage form in his stomach, and that enraged him further—the fact that she still had the power to affect him after all these years.

His shoulders tensed. 'Or perhaps they have their own agenda.'

Teddie felt a rush of anger spread over her skin like a heat rash. '*Nobody* has been giving me advice. I make my own decisions—although I wouldn't expect you to understand that.' Heart thumping, she lifted her gaze to his. 'It was always a difficult concept for you, wasn't it, Aristo? My being an independent woman?'

His eyes flickered, and she could almost see the fuse inside of him catch light.

'If by "independent" you mean self-absorbed and unsupportive, then, yes, I suppose it was.'

She caught her breath. The room felt suddenly cramped and airless, as though it had shrunk in the face of his anger—an anger which fed the outrage that had been simmering inside her since meeting him earlier.

'*You're* calling *me* self-absorbed and unsupportive?' She glared at him, the sheer injustice of his statement blowing her away. She could feel her grip on her temper starting to slip. How dare he turn up here, in her home, and start throwing accusations at her?

But even as she choked on her anger, she wasn't really surprised. Back when she'd loved him, she'd known that he had a single-minded vision of the world—a world in which he was always in the right and always had the last word. Her refusing to talk to him now simply didn't fit with that expectation.

Her motives, her needs, were irrelevant. As far as he was concerned she had merely issued him with a challenge that must instantly be confronted and crushed.

Queasily, she remembered his cold hostility when she'd refused to give up her job. Was that when their marriage had really ended? It was certainly the moment when she'd finally been forced to acknowledge the facts. That marrying Aristo had not been an act of impulse, driven by an undeniable love, but a mistake based on a misguided hope and longing to have a place in his life, and in his heart.

But Aristo didn't have a heart, and he hadn't come to her apartment to return a pack of cards. As usual, he just wanted to have the last word.

Crossing her arms to contain the ache in her chest, she lifted her chin. 'If you believe that, then perhaps I should have given you the number for my doctor, as you're clearly delusional,' she snapped. 'Wanting to carry on doing a job I loved didn't make me self-absorbed, Aristo. It was an act of self-preservation.'

Aristo stared at her, his shoulders rigid with frustration. 'Self-preservation!' he scoffed. 'You were living in a penthouse in Manhattan with a view of Central Park. You were hardly on Skid Row.' He shook his dark head in disbelief. 'That's the trouble with you, Teddie—you're so used to performing you turn every single part of your life into a stunt, even this conversation.'

They were both almost shouting now, their bodies braced against the incoming storm.

Her eyes narrowed. 'You think this is a conversation?' she snapped. 'You didn't come here to converse. I bruised your ego so you wanted—'

'Mommy—Mommy!'

The child's voice came from somewhere behind her, cutting through her angry tirade like a scythe through wheat. Turning instantly, instinctively, Teddie cleared her throat.

'Oh, sweetheart, it's all right.'

Her son, George, blinked up at her. He was wearing his pyjamas and holding his favourite toy boat and she felt a rush of pure, fierce love as she looked down into his huge, anxious dark eyes.

'Mommy shouted...'

He bit his lip and, hearing the wobble in his voice, she reached down and curved her arm unsteadily around his stocky little waist and pulled him closer, pressing his body against hers. 'I'm sorry, darling. Did Mommy wake you?'

Lifting him up, she held him tightly as he nodded his head against her shoulder.

Watching Teddie press her face against the little dark-haired boy's cheek, Aristo felt his stomach turn to ice.

He felt winded by the discovery that she had a child. No, it was more than that: he felt *wounded*, even though he could come up with no rational explanation for why that should be the case.

His pulse was racing like a bolting horse, his thoughts firing off in every direction. He could hardly take it in, but there could be no mistake. This child was Teddie's son. But why hadn't she told him?

Thinking back to their earlier conversation, he replayed her words and felt an icy fury rise up inside of him. Not only had she said nothing, she'd lied to his face when he'd asked her about her family. Of course he'd been talking about siblings, cousins, aunts—but why hadn't she told him then? Why had she kept her son a secret?

At that moment the little boy lifted his face and suddenly he couldn't breathe. At the periphery of his vision he could see Teddie turning to face him, and then he knew why, for her green eyes were telling him what her mouth—that beautiful, soft, deceiving mouth—had failed to do earlier.

This was his son.

Like a drowning man, he saw his whole life speeding through his head—meeting Teddie at that dinner, her long dark hair swinging forward half-hiding a smile that had stolen his breath away, the echoing emptiness of his apartment, and that moment in the Kildare when she'd hesitated...

He breathed out unsteadily, and abruptly his pulse juddered to a halt.

Only, he wasn't drowning in water, but in lies. Teddie's lies.

The resentment and hostility he'd felt after she'd left him, the shock of bumping into her today—all of it was swept aside in a firestorm of fury so blindingly white and intense that he had to reach out and steady himself against a bookcase.

But the luxury of losing his temper with Teddie would have to wait. Right now it was time to meet his son.

'I'm sorry too,' he said gently, making sure that none of the emotions roiling inside his head were audible in his voice as he smiled at his son for the first time.

'But you don't need to worry.' Skewering Teddie with his gaze, he took a step closer. 'Mommy and I are going to have a chat, aren't we?'

He turned to Teddie, making sure that the smooth blandness of his voice in no way detracted from the blistering rage in his eyes. Hearing her small, sharp intake of breath, he felt the glacier in his chest start to scrape forward. It had been barely audible, but it was all the confirmation he needed.

Forcing herself to meet his gaze, Teddie nodded mechanically, but inside her head a mantra of panic-stricken thoughts was beating in time to her heartbeat. *He knows. He knows George is his son. What am I going to do?*

Clearing her throat, she smiled. 'Yes, that's right. We're going to have a grown-ups talk. And you, young man, are going to be taken back to bed.'

Although, given that her legs felt as though they were made of blancmange, that might be easier to say than do.

Aristo stared at her coldly. 'But not before you've introduced me, of course.'

Her chin jerked up, but his glittering gaze silenced her words of objection.

'This is my son, George,' she said stiffly.

'Hello, George.' Aristo smiled. 'I'm very honoured to meet you. My name is Aristo Leonidas, and I'm an old friend of your mommy's.'

Gazing into his son's eyes—dark eyes that were almost identical in shape and colour to his own—he felt his stomach tighten painfully. George had his jawline and his high cheekbones; the likeness between them was remarkable, undeniable. At the same age they would have looked like twins.

As George smiled uncertainly back at him he felt almost blinded with outrage at Teddie's deceit. His son must be three years old. How much had he missed during that time? First tooth. First word. First steps. Holidays and birthdays. And in the future, what other occasions would he have unknowingly not attended—graduation, wedding day...

He gritted his teeth.

Maybe he'd not actually thought about becoming a father, but Teddie had unilaterally taken away his right to be one. How was he ever going to make good the time he'd missed? No, not *missed*, he thought savagely. Teddie had cheated him of three years of his son's life. Worse, not only had she deliberately kept his son a secret from him for all that time, she had clearly been planning to keep him in ignorance of George's existence for ever.

Hell, she'd even lied to him tonight, telling him that he had to be quiet because of her elderly neighbours.

Glancing up, he refocused on his son's face and, seeing the confusion in George's eyes, pushed his anger away. 'I know you're not ready to shake hands yet and that's a good thing, because we need to get to know each other a bit better first. But maybe we could just bump knuckles for now.'

Raising his hand, he curled his fingers into a fist, his heart contracting as his son copied him, and they gently bumped fists.

'Hey, what's that? Is that a boat?' Aristo watched as George uncurled his fingers.

'It's my boat,' he said solemnly.

'I love your boat.' Aristo glanced at it admiringly. 'I have a real boat like that. Maybe you could come for a ride on it with Mommy. Would you like that?'

George nodded, and Teddie felt her chest hollow out with panic.

Watching the sudden intimacy between her ex-husband and their son, she felt something wrench apart inside her, for the two of them were so close—not just physically but in their very likeness. It was both touching and terrifying, almost overwhelmingly so.

Clearing her throat, she smiled stiffly. 'That would be lovely, wouldn't it, George? Right now though, it really is time to go back to bed.'

In his bedroom, she tucked him under his duvet,

keeping up a steady stream of chatter until his eyelids fluttered shut.

If only she could just crawl in beside him and close her eyes too. Remembering the look on Aristo's face as he'd worked out that George was his son, she felt her pulse begin beating in her neck like a moth against glass. Despite his outer calm, she knew that he was angry—more angry than she had ever seen him, more angry than she could have imagined possible.

Not that she could blame him, she thought, guilt scraping over her skin like sandpaper. Had their roles been reversed she would have been just as furious. And the fact that part of her had always wanted to tell him the truth didn't feel like much of a defence.

She really should be relieved, though, for it had been getting harder and harder to keep lying.

But now she would have to pay the price for those lies and face his anger. That was bad enough, but more terrifying still was the sudden knife-twist of realisation that Aristo had both a moral *and* a legal right to be in his son's life. It didn't matter about their divorce. George was his son, and if he wanted to press that point home he had the power and the money to do so emphatically—not just here in her apartment but in court.

The thought of facing Aristo in court made her want to throw up.

So face him now, she ordered herself. And, taking a deep breath, she stood up and made her way back to the living room.

He swung round towards her, and her heart began beating so fast she thought it would burst through her ribs. She had thought he was angry before, but clearly each minute that had passed during her absence had increased his fury exponentially, so that now, as he walked towards her, it was the arctic blast of his contempt that held her frozen to the spot.

'I knew you were shallow and unscrupulous,' he said, his eyes gleaming like black ice, 'but at what point exactly did your morals become so skewed that you decided to keep my son a secret from me?'

'That's not fair—'

His black eyes slammed into hers. '*Fair?* You're really quite something, Teddie. I thought you just stole money from me. Turns out you stole my son.'

'I didn't steal him—' she began, but he cut her off.

'Oh, I'm sure you've post-rationalised it. What did you tell yourself? *What he doesn't know won't hurt him?*' he imitated her voice. *'It'll be for the best.'*

'I did do it for the best.' Her voice was shaking, but her eyes were level with his. 'I did what was best *for me*, Aristo, because there was only me.'

He felt his breathing jerk. 'Not true. You had a husband.'

'*Ex*-husband,' she snapped. 'We were divorced by then. Not that it would have made any difference. You were never there.'

His eyes didn't leave hers. 'You really can't help yourself, can you? It's just lie after lie after lie.'

Teddie swallowed. It was true—she had lied repeatedly. But not because she'd wanted to and not about the past. It wasn't fair of Aristo to judge her with hindsight. He might be in shock now, but she'd had just the same shock four years ago when, thanks to him, she'd been homeless and alone.

'I was going to tell you—' She broke off as he laughed, the bitterness reverberating around the small room.

'Of course you were.'

'I didn't mean now—today. I meant in the future.'

'The future?' He repeated the word slowly, as though not quite sure of its meaning. 'What's wrong with the present? What was wrong with this morning?'

'It all happened so quickly.' She looked at him defensively. 'I wasn't expecting to see you.'

Aristo stared at her in disbelief. 'And that's a reason, is it? Reason enough for my son to grow up without a father? Or have you got some surrogate daddy in mind? Is that why you ran out on me this morning?'

The thought stung. He might not have been celibate, but dating—certainly anything serious—had been the last thing on his mind for the past four years. Work—in particular the expansion of his empire, and more recently his upcoming flotation on the stock exchange—had taken up so much of his time and energy. On those occasions when he'd needed a 'plus-one', he been careful to keep her at a distance.

Clearly Teddie had found him far easier to replace.

His eyes narrowed. 'I mean, it's just what you *do*, isn't it, Teddie? That's your real act! Not all this nonsense.' He held up the box of cards. 'You set it all up.' *Set me up*, he thought savagely. 'Then take what you want and move on.'

'If you're talking about our marriage, I had plenty of reasons to leave. And I didn't take anything.'

She felt a sudden sharp pang of guilt as she thought of her son—*their* son—but then she repeated his sneering reference to her work as 'nonsense' inside her head, and pushed her guilt aside.

Glaring at him, she shook her head, whipping her dark hair like a horse swatting flies with its tail. 'And not that it's any of your business but there is no man in my life, and there's certainly no daddy in George's.'

The outrage in her voice sounded real, and he

wanted to believe her for his pride's sake, if nothing else. But, aside from the faint flush of colour creeping over her cheeks, she had already told so many different lies in such a short space of time that it was hard to believe anything she said. Clearly lying was second nature to her.

His heart was suddenly speeding and his skin felt cool and clammy with shock—not just at finding out he was a father, but at how ruthlessly Teddie had played him.

'So let me get this clear,' he said slowly. 'At some unspecified point in the future you were planning on telling me about my son?'

Teddie hesitated. If only she could plead the Fifth Amendment but this was one question that required an answer. Actually, it required the truth.

'I don't know. Honestly, most days I'm just trying to deal with the day-to-day of work and being a mom to George.'

And grieving for the man I loved and lost.

Blocking off the memories of those terrible weeks and months after they'd split, she cleared her throat. 'We were already divorced by the time I found out I was pregnant. We weren't talking, and you weren't even in the country.'

His eyes bored into eyes. 'And so you just unilaterally decided to disappear into thin air with my child? He's my *son*—not some prop in your magic show.'

Stung, and shocked by the level of emotion in his voice, she said defensively, 'I know and I'm sorry.'

He swore under his breath. 'Sorry is not enough, Teddie. I have a child, and I fully intend to get to know him.'

It wasn't an outright threat, more a statement of intent, but she could see that his shock at discovering he was a father was fading and in its place was that familiar need to take control of the situation.

She felt a ripple of apprehension run down her backbone. Where did that leave her?

Last time she and Aristo had gone head to head she'd been cast out from his kingdom, her unimportance in his life no longer just a private fear but an actuality.

But four years ago she'd been young and in love, unsure of her place in the world. Now, though, she was a successful businesswoman and a hands-on single mother—and, most important of all, she understood what she'd been too naive and too dazzled to see four years ago.

Aristo had no capacity for or interest in emotional ties. She'd learned that first-hand over six agonising months spent watching his obsession with work consume their marriage and exclude her from his life.

She brought her eyes back to his. Yes, she should have told him the truth, but he'd given her no reason to do so—no reason other than biology for her to allow him into George's life.

And now? Maybe if Aristo had been a different kind of man she would have caved, but she knew that no matter how insistent he was now about wanting to get to know their son, it was only a matter of time before he lost interest—like her own father had. But George would not grow up as she had, feeling as though he was at the bottom of his father's agenda.

'*Our* son is not some chess piece you can move about on a board to suit you, Aristo. He's a person with feelings and needs—'

He cut her off. 'Yes, he is, and he needs to see me—his father.'

Folding her arms, Teddie glared at him, anger leaping over her skin in pulses. 'He needs consistency and security—not somebody offering him trips on a speedboat and then disappearing for days.'

He shook his head dismissively. 'I'm standing right here, Teddie.'

'For how long?' she countered. 'A day? A week? I mean, when exactly *is* your next business trip?'

His jaw tightened. 'That is irrelevant.'

'No, it's not. I'm being realistic about your limitations.'

Looking away, she clenched her fists. And her limitations. Her life might be bereft of romance and passion, but it was peaceful. The thought of having Aristo flitting in and out of her and George's life was just too unbearable to contemplate.

'I have rights, Teddie,' he said quietly, and something in his voice pulled her gaze back to his face. 'I'm guessing you can live with ignoring that fact—you've managed it for four years. But George has rights too, and I'm wondering what's going to happen when he realises that he has a father—a father you kept at arm's length. Can you live with that?'

Teddie stared at him, her heart pounding, hating him for finding the weakness in her argument.

'Fine,' she snapped, her hands balling into fists. 'You can see him.' But it was absolutely, definitely *not* going to be in her apartment. 'I suggest we find somewhere neutral.'

'Neutral—that's an interesting euphemism.'

He suddenly sounded amused, and she felt her pulse accelerate as she realised that his anger seemed to have faded and he was now watching her intently in a way that made her breathing come to a sudden, swift stop.

'If you're trying to find a place where you and I will feel "neutral" about one another, then I think you might need a bigger planet. Maybe a different solar system.'

She swallowed. His words were reverberating inside her head, bumping into memories so explicit and uncensored that she had to curl her fingers into her palms to stop her hands shaking.

'I don't know what you're talking about,' she said hoarsely, trying her hardest not to notice the way her stomach was clenching.

She felt heat break out over her skin as he took a step towards her.

'Yes, you do, Teddie. I'm talking about sex. And about how, despite all this, you still want me and I still want you.'

An ache like hunger, only more insistent, shot through her and she stared at him, her green eyes widening in shock at the bluntness of his statement.

He raised an eyebrow. 'What? Are you going to lie about that too?' He shook his head dismissively. 'Then you're a coward as well as a liar.'

'I'm not a coward,' she snapped. 'I just don't happen to agree with your unnecessary and rather crude remark.'

His dark eyes locked onto hers and she knew that this time her lie might as well be written in block capitals across her forehead.

'Yes, you do. You're just scared that you feel this way. Scared that you want me.'

Teddie breathed out shakily. He was close now—close enough for her to see the tiny flecks of grey and gold in the inky pools of his eyes. Close enough that she could smell his clean, masculine scent. So close that she could not just see the curves of muscle beneath his sweater but reach out and touch them—

'You're so arrogant.'

He took another step closer and lifted his hand. Her pulse fluttered as he traced the curve of her jaw with his thumb.

'And you're so beautiful, but neither of those statements changes the facts.'

She could feel his gaze seeking hers and, looking up, she saw that his eyes were shimmering with an emotion she recognised and understood—because she was feeling it too.

'Like it or not, we still burn for one another, and I know you feel it too. There's a connection between us.'

She stared at him, hypnotised not just by the truth of his words but by the slow, steady pulse of heat in her blood. And then, in a split second of clarity, she saw herself, saw his hand capturing her face, saw where it was heading, and was instantly maddened by his audacity and ashamed of her weakness.

Jerking her head away from his hand, she lifted her chin. 'You're wrong, Aristo. It's all in your head. It's not real,' she lied again.

He stared at her, his gaze taking in her flushed cheeks and the pulse beating at the base of her throat. 'Not real?' he softly. 'It looks pretty real from where I'm standing.'

Her whole body throbbing, she breathed out unsteadily. 'That's magic for you, Aristo. It plays tricks with the senses…makes you believe in the impossible. And you and I are impossible.' Fixing her green eyes on her ex-husband's breathtakingly handsome face, she gave him a small, tight smile. 'You being George's father changes nothing between us.'

His expression was unreadable, but as his dark, knowing gaze locked with hers she knew that she wasn't fooling either of them, and his next comment reinforced that fact.

'You're right, it doesn't,' he said into the tense silence. 'So perhaps from now on we can both stop playing games.'

He took a step backwards, his satisfied expression making her heart thump against her chest.

'I'll call you, but if in the meantime you want me desperately…'

Eyes gleaming, he reached into his jacket and held out a small white card. 'That's my number.'

'Well, I won't be calling it,' she snapped. 'As the chances of me wanting you "desperately" are less than zero.'

He smiled. 'Of course they are.'

She wanted to throw his remark back in his face, to claim that he was reading the signals all wrong, but before she had the chance to think of a suitably withering response he turned and strolled out of the room with the same swagger with which he'd entered it.

Heart pounding, she waited until she was sure that he'd left the building before darting across the room to close and bolt the door. Only, like the stable door, it was too late, she thought as she sank down onto her sofa with legs that were still unsteady. She'd not only let him back into her home, but into her life.

CHAPTER THREE

WALKING INTO HIS APARTMENT, Aristo stared blankly across the gleaming modern interior, a stream of disconnected, equally frustrating thoughts jamming his brain. He'd barely registered the hour-long drive home from Teddie's apartment. Instead he'd been preoccupied by that simmering undercurrent of attraction between them.

They'd both been so angry, and yet even beneath the fury he had felt it, strumming and intensifying like the vibrating rails beneath an express train.

Of course he'd known it was there since this morning—from that moment when he'd turned around in the Kildare and his stomach had gone into freefall. It had been like watching flashes of lightning on the horizon: you knew a storm was heading your way.

And he'd wanted the storm to come—and so had Teddie—right up until she'd told him that it was all in his head.

Not that he'd believed her. It had been just one more lie in a day of lies.

He breathed out slowly, trying to shift the memory of her final stinging remark to him.

'You and I are impossible. You being George's father changes nothing between us.'

Wrong, he thought irritably. It changed everything.

No matter how much she wanted to deny it, there *was* a connection between them—and it wasn't just based on sex, he thought, his heart tightening as he remembered his son bumping fists with him.

He still couldn't believe that he was a father. A *father*!

The word kept repeating inside his head like a scratched record.

Suddenly he needed a drink!

In the cavernous stainless steel and polished concrete kitchen, he poured himself a glass of red wine and made his way to the rooftop terrace that led off the living area.

Collapsing into a chair, he gazed moodily out at the New York skyline. Even from so high up he could feel the city's energy rising up like a wave, but for once he didn't respond to its power. He was too busy trying to piece together the life that Teddie had shattered when she'd walked into his hotel.

And if that hadn't been enough of a shock, she'd then lobbed a grenade into his perfectly ordered world in the shape of a three-year-old son.

Welcome to fatherhood, Teddie-Taylor style.

Thanks to her, he'd gone from nought to being the father of a miniature version of himself in a matter of seconds, with Teddie presenting George to him like the proverbial rabbit being pulled from a hat.

He ran his hand slowly over his face, as though it might smooth the disarray of his thoughts. It felt surreal to be contemplating even the concept of being a father, let alone the reality. He'd never really imagined having a child—not out of any deep-rooted opposition to being a father, but because work and the expansion of his business empire required all his energy and focus.

He frowned. But maybe there were other reasons too? Could his father's decision to opt out of his responsibilities have made him question his own programming for parenthood? Possibly, he decided after a moment's thought. Apostolos Leonidas had been an intermittent and largely reluctant presence in his life, and maybe he had just assumed that he'd be the same.

And up until now he'd more or less given his father a free pass—having been made to look a fool, his father had understandably wanted nothing to do with his adulterous wife, and that had meant having nothing to do with his son either.

But even when Aristo had been blinded with shock and anger earlier he'd felt no resentment towards George, no sense of panic or dismay. Gazing down into his son's dark eyes, he had felt his heart tighten in recognition—and love.

His shoulders stiffened. The same love that Teddie clearly felt for George?

Resentment still simmered inside him, but he couldn't stop himself from reluctantly admiring his ex-wife. Whatever else she might be, Teddie was a good mother. George clearly adored her, and she loved their son—not with his own mother's chilly, grudging variety of love, nor the nod of recognition that had passed for love in his father's head. Just love—pure, simple and unselfish.

Imagining how it must feel to be the focus of that kind of affection and tenderness, he felt something tauten inside him—not just a sense of responsibility, but of resolve. He was George's father, and it was his job to make sure his son had the love and security that he himself had been denied as a child.

His parents' divorce and subsequent remarriages had left him rootless and unsure of his place in the world, and he knew instinctively that George needed both his parents. But if that was to happen then this time Teddie wouldn't be running anywhere—ever. Only, judging by how quickly she had bolted from his life last time, he needed to make that clear sooner rather than later.

'Well, if you ask me, it could have been a lot worse.'

Elliot raised his elbows swiftly off the breakfast bar as Teddie swept past him with a wet cloth, cleaning the evidence of George's cereal from the surface and wishing she could wipe Aristo from her life just as effortlessly.

Elliot hadn't appeared the night before but had arrived at breakfast, bringing doughnuts and his usual reassuring patter, and she'd been both grateful and relieved to see him.

It wasn't that he could do anything to change what had happened, but he made her feel calmer, more rational. Less like the woman she'd been last night.

Her fingers tightened around the cloth and she closed her eyes.

That, in short, was the problem. Maybe it was because he was so uncompromisingly masculine physically, but Aristo made her feel like a woman—fierce and wild and hungry to touch and be touched. They'd felt so right together; he'd felt so right against her. And, even though she despised herself for being so shallow, she couldn't pretend that anything had changed. When he was near her she was still so aware of his body, his breathing, the heat of his skin...

Her insides felt suddenly hot and tight and, breathing out a little, she opened her eyes. She'd done everything she could to excise the memory of what it felt like to be held in Aristo's arms, only for him to turn up on her doorstep and make a mockery of all her efforts. It wasn't fair—but that didn't mean she was going to roll over and let him turn her and George's lives upside down.

'It could?' Turning, she stared at Elliot disbelief. 'How, Elliot? How could it be worse?'

He shrugged, his expression innocent. 'He could have kissed you.'

Remembering how close she'd come to letting that happen, she scowled at him, a blush of colour heating her cheeks. 'He didn't.'

'Or you could have kissed him— Hey, it was a joke.' Grinning, he caught the cloth that Teddie threw at him. 'Where's your sense of humour?'

Collapsing onto the stool beside him, she shook her head. 'It packed its bags and left shortly after Aristotle Leonidas arrived.'

She felt a sudden rush of panic, remembering that stand-off between them—the prickling of her skin and the intensity of his gaze, his dark eyes scanning her face, all-seeing, hungry, unwavering… Her stomach tightened, her hands curling into fists. She might not have given in last night, but this thing, this 'connection' between them wasn't going to just disappear.

But she could.

The thought popped into her head unbidden, fully formed, because of course that was still her gut instinct. Before Aristo, years of her life had been spent living out of suitcases, staying in hotels and motels, always ready to leave, to flee like a getaway driver after a heist. Running away had been her quick fix, her go-to solution for dealing with any problem in her life, any time things got hard.

It was a hangover from a childhood spent dodging unpaid bills and bailiffs and a legacy from her father—not that she'd ever thought of him as that. Wyatt Taylor had never stayed around long enough for the name 'Dad' to stick. Just long enough to teach her a couple of magic tricks and to make her miss him when he left.

Her heart began to pound.

Only, how could she run with a child? George's life was here, in New York. He went to nursery here, he had friends, a routine. He was the reason she'd stopped running.

As though sensing her panic, Elliot reached over and pushed a stray strand of hair away from her face.

'Come on, Teddie, I know he was a pig to you, and maybe it wasn't ideal, him turning up here out of the blue, but…' He hesitated, his expression becoming uncharacteristically serious. 'But whatever you're telling yourself, you're wrong. You can't run this time, babe.'

As she glanced up guiltily he gave her a lop-sided smile.

'I've known you since I was twelve years old. I don't need supernatural powers to read your mind.

This isn't something you can run away from, and deep down I don't think you really want to.'

She lifted her chin, narrowing her green eyes. 'And yet strangely, on a superficial level, I feel completely certain that I absolutely do.'

Elliot poked one of her clenched hands with his finger. 'No, you don't. I was there, remember? I know how often you tried to call him. I know how many messages you left, how upset you were.' His jaw tensed. 'I'm no fan of Aristotle Leonidas, but—' he frowned '—he's still George's father and he's got a right to see his son. Right now it's a shock, but once you get used to the idea it'll be okay, I promise. I mean, loads of couples share custody of their children.'

Teddie gave him a small, tight smile.

Thinking about a future in which she would have to see Aristo on a regular basis, speak to him and have him turning up on her doorstep, was not her definition of okay. But maybe over time her feelings for him would diminish, like radioactivity—only didn't that take, like, decades? Not that it mattered how she felt, or where she was. She could run but, as Elliot said, she couldn't hide from the truth any more. Aristo was George's father and she was just going to have to suck it up.

Pushing back his stool, Elliot stood up. 'I gotta go, but I'll call you later.' Sliding his arms into his jacket, he kissed her forehead. 'And don't worry.

Leopards don't change their spots, baby, and from everything you've ever told me about your ex he's not the kind to stick around long enough for this to become a problem.'

Watching Elliot let himself out of the apartment, she knew he was trying to reassure her. And she should feel reassured—it was, after all, what she wanted, wasn't it? For Aristo to disappear from her life for good? Only, for some strange reason, that thought didn't seem quite comforting as she'd imagined it would.

While George took his afternoon nap Teddie tidied the apartment, moving automatically to pick up the tiny toy cars and miniature dinosaurs that were scattered everywhere. Eventually she stopped beside her bed and, kneeling down, pulled out a cardboard box.

Feeling a lump start to build in her throat, she hesitated, and then sat on the floor. Lifting off the lid, she gazed down at the contents.

Was that it? Had her marriage really amounted to nothing more than a shoebox shoved under a bed?

Pushing aside the letters and documents, she reached to the bottom of the box and pulled out a small blue box.

Her hand twitched and then slowly, heart thumping erratically, she opened it and stared down at the plain gold band. For a moment she couldn't move, but as her breathing steadied she picked up her wedding ring and slid it onto her finger.

She still wasn't sure why she had kept it. But the answer to that was not as simple as the question implied.

At first, in the weeks after she'd moved out of Aristo's apartment—and it had always felt like *his* apartment—she'd kept wearing it because even though it had become clear to her by then that her husband was a different person from the impulsive lover she'd promised to love and honour and cherish, she hadn't been ready to give up on her marriage.

And then later it had been the one thing he'd given to her that he hadn't and could never take away—of course that had been before she found out about George.

Her throat tightened. She could still picture the exact moment that she'd finally decided to stop wearing it.

It had been on the taxi ride home from that night she'd spent in Aristo's arms, hoping and believing that they'd been given a second chance.

He'd followed her out of their meeting with the lawyers earlier and they'd argued, both of them simmering with fury, and then they'd looked into each other's eyes and desire had been stronger than their anger combined. Unreasonable, but undeniable.

But then what did desire ever have to do with reason?

They'd rented a hotel room like newlyweds, kissing and pulling at each other's clothes in the lift, hardly noticing the other guests' shocked or amused expressions as they'd run to their room.

But even before the sheets tangled around their warm, damp bodies had grown cold she'd realised her mistake.

That night hadn't been some eleventh-hour reprieve for their marriage. Aristo hadn't acknowledged his part in their marital problems, or been willing to listen to her point of view. Instead he'd just wanted to get his own way and, having failed to convince her with words he'd switched tactics. Like the hopeless, lovestruck fool she had been then, she'd let herself be persuaded by the softness of his mouth and the hard length of his body.

But, waking in the strange bed, she'd realised her mistake instantly.

She breathed out unsteadily, remembering how his face had grown hard and expressionless, the post-coital tenderness in his eyes fading as he'd told that he'd pay for the room, but that would be the last dollar she'd see of his money.

It hadn't been. Three weeks later she'd emptied one of the bank accounts they'd shared—the one with the least amount of money in it—partly to prove him wrong, but mostly so his unborn child would have something from its father.

Sliding the ring off her finger, she put it back in the box and got slowly to her feet. Elliot was right. She needed to face reality, and it would be easier to do so if she was in control of what was happening rather than sitting and stewing, waiting for Aristo to call.

Walking back into the living room, she picked up the card he'd given her the night before and punched out his number on her mobile before she had the chance to change her mind.

'Hello, Teddie.'

She hadn't expected him to pick up quite so quickly, or to know it was her, but that wasn't why she slid down onto the sofa. It was just that hearing his voice down the phone again felt strangely intimate, and for a split second she was reminded of how they'd used to talk when they'd first met. Conversations in the early hours of the morning after she'd finished performing and she was lying in bed in some hotel on the other side of the country.

It hadn't mattered what time she'd called—he'd always answered and they'd talked sometimes for hours. She felt her skin prickle. And not just talk... Sometimes he'd made up stories to help her fall asleep.

Curling her fingers around the phone, she gripped it more tightly. Remembering Aristo doing that for her was like waking to find a handcuff around her wrist, linking her to him in a way she hadn't imagined.

Steadying her breathing, she pushed the memory to the back of her mind. 'We need to talk,' she said bluntly. 'About George.'

'So talk.'

'No, not on the phone. We need to meet.'

There was a short pause, and her chest tightened as she imagined him leaning back in his chair, a small triumphant smile curving his mouth.

'I can come to your apartment.'

'No.' Hearing the panic in her voice, she frowned. But there was no way he was coming to the apartment again, not after what nearly happened last time. 'I'll come to your office.'

She glanced at the time. She could drop George off at Elliot's and then go on into Manhattan.

'Shall we say about five?'

'I look forward to it,' he said softly.

At exactly five o'clock she was staring up at a tall, gleaming tower as all around her crowds of tourists chatted and laughed—no doubt on their way to see the Empire State Building or some other world-famous landmark.

If only she was a tourist too, enjoying a well-earned holiday, instead of having to face her clever, calculating ex-husband. But the sooner she faced

Aristo the sooner she could return home, and so, heart pounding, she slipped through the revolving doors into the cool smoked glass interior of the Leonidas Holdings' headquarters.

Five minutes later she was riding up in an elevator, only just managing to force her mouth into a stiff smile as the doors opened.

'Ms Taylor.' Smiling politely, a young male assistant stepped forward. 'If you'd like to come with me, Mr Leonidas' office is this way.'

But not Mr Leonidas, Teddie discovered as the assistant showed her into the empty office. She wondered if Aristo had absented himself on purpose. Probably, she decided. No doubt he was trying to psyche her out by making her wait, by giving her a glimpse of his personal fiefdom.

She glanced slowly around the room, her narrowed gaze taking in the dazzling panoramic views of New York, the Bauhaus furniture and the huge abstract painting that hung behind his desk.

'Sorry to keep you waiting.'

She turned, her body tensing automatically as Aristo strolled into the room, his dark eyes sweeping assessingly over her black cigarette trousers, burgundy silk shirt and towering stiletto heels.

He stopped in front of her and she felt her stomach flip over. He'd taken off his jacket, and the sleeves of his cornflower-blue shirt were rolled up, the collar loosened. Her eyes darted involuntarily between the triangle of golden skin at the base of his neck and the fine dark hair on his forearms.

Her breath pedalled inside her chest. He looked both invincible and stupidly sexy, and any hope she'd had that she might have miraculously developed an immunity to him in the intervening hours since she'd seen him evaporated like early-morning mist. Even just being in the same space as him was sending her body haywire, her chest constricting and a prickling heat spreading like a forest fire over her skin.

If Aristo was feeling as uncomfortable as she was, he wasn't showing it. But then in the six months of their marriage she'd never really known what he was thinking—she might be a mistress of illusion on stage, but he was a master at disguising his feelings. Her lips tightened. Although that, of course, presupposed that he had any.

'It's fine,' she said stiffly. 'I know you're a busy man.'

His gaze hovered over her face and she cursed herself silently, for she knew what he was thinking.

Aristo's obsession with work had quickly become an issue for her. The long hours he'd spent at the office and his single-minded focus on building his business had slowly but inevitably excluded her from his life. Not that either of them had done much to stop it eroding their marriage. For Aristo it had only ever been *her* problem, and she had found it impossible to tell him the truth. That she wanted the man who had craved her, who had been so hungry to share her life that he hadn't been willing to wait.

She swallowed, pushing back against the sudden swell of misery spreading through her. It was her own fault. She should have known what to expect when he'd cut their honeymoon short to fly halfway across the world to buy a resort. But of course when he'd pulled her into his arms and told her it was a one-off she'd believed him. She'd wanted to believe him, and to believe that she hadn't just made the biggest mistake of her life.

Only, her brief doomed marriage was not what she wanted to talk about now. They'd moved way past the point where there was even a 'them' to discuss. As far as she was concerned, the less she had to do with him the better, and after this meeting hopefully there would be no reason for her to see him except briefly and occasionally.

Watching the conflicting emotions flitting across his ex-wife's face, Aristo felt a ripple of frustration. She had always been so unsupportive of his career, when all he'd been trying to do was build a life for her, for them.

Glancing round his office, he steadied his breathing. Surely now she could understand what he'd been trying to do? But, either way, he wasn't going to let it get in the way of what really mattered.

He shrugged. 'Very busy,' he said softly. 'But let's not get distracted. I'm sure you didn't come here to talk about my work.'

She gave him a small, tight smile. 'We need to make arrangements. Something stable and uncomplicated. Because what's most important to me is that George feels happy and safe.'

He nodded. 'And I want that too.' Gesturing towards a cluster of easy chairs and a sofa grouped in front of the windows, he smiled slowly. 'So, why don't we sit down and talk about how we can make that happen?'

Teddie gazed at him warily. So far it was all going better than she'd expected. Her heartbeat scuttled forward. Only, it wasn't fair of him to smile like that. It would be so much easier for her to keep a clear head if he was cold and dismissive. When he smiled that extraordinary smile it was difficult to think straight. Difficult to think about anything other than that beautiful mouth.

Feeling his dark gaze, she ignored both his hand and the sudden rapid pounding of her heart and nodded, then walked as casually as she could manage across the room.

She purposely avoided the sofa and sat down in one of the chairs, but regretted her decision almost immediately as, dropping down into the chair closest to hers, he stretched out his long, muscular legs and began to speak.

'Look, Teddie, before we start I have something I need to say to you.'

'So say it.' She had been aiming to sound casual, offhand. Instead, though, her voice sounded stiff and unnatural.

His eyes fixed on hers. 'I know this can't be easy, having me back in your life and in George's life. But I'm going to try to make it as painless and unproblematic as possible for both of us. All I want is to be a good father.'

She held his gaze. It was on the tip of her tongue to tell him that he *wasn't* back in her life. But to be fair he was trying to meet her halfway, and it seemed churlish to nit-pick over his choice of words.

Glancing away to the skyline, she shrugged. 'I hope so. That's why I'm here.'

It was true, and she wanted to believe Aristo, to take his words at face-value—only after everything he'd said and done in the past it was just so hard to trust him. But if this was going to work, for her son's sake, she was going to have to put the past behind her and concentrate on the present.

She took a quick, steadying breath and said quickly, 'I know it probably doesn't seem like it to you, but I really do want George to get to know you.'

The air seemed to still, like a held breath, and, looking up, she found Aristo watching her so steadily and intently that for a moment she forgot where she was. Suddenly the huge office seemed as though it had shrunk, and his body seemed way too close to hers.

Before she could stop herself she shifted in her seat, drawing her legs in tighter and then regretting it immediately as his eyes dropped to her throat, taking in the jerkiness of her pulse.

'So what do you suggest?'

It was a straightforward enough question, and his expression was blandly innocent, but something in his eyes made her body tense, her muscles popping and suddenly primed for flight as she quickly went through the options she'd rehearsed on her journey to his office.

'I thought perhaps we could meet in a park,' she said hopefully. 'George loves swings, and we have a nice park just down the street.'

She felt her pulse begin to hopscotch forward as slowly he shook his head.

'I was thinking of something more than just a trip to the swings. How about you bring George to the apartment for a weekend? That way we'll have more time, and plenty of space, and of course there's the pool.' He raised his dark gaze to hers. 'You *have* taught him to swim?'

She glared at him. 'Yes, of course I have. But—'

'Excellent, so we're agreed.' His smile widened but she started to shake her head.

'No, Aristo. We are not agreed.' She gritted her teeth. How had she ever thought this would be easy?

'Then I'll come to yours,' he said coolly.

Her back stiffened. He absolutely definitely wasn't coming to her apartment, and nor did she want to go to back to the apartment that had once been her home, with all its many reminders of their shared past.

So tell him what you do want then, she told herself.

'I don't think that's a good idea.' She spoke quickly, trying to inject a businesslike tone into her voice.

'No? But you do want to *arrange* something, right?'

He lounged back, his arm resting easily against the side of the chair, and suddenly she wanted to reach out and touch the golden skin, run her fingertips over the smooth curve of muscle pressing against the fabric of his shirt.

'Yes—yes, of course I do.' She dragged her eyes away, up to the compelling dark eyes and dangerous curves of his face.

He nodded. 'Something stable and uncomplicated, I think you said.'

'Yes, that's what I want, but...' She gazed at him

uncertainly, wondering exactly where the conversation was going.

'Then the solution is staring us in the face.'

He went on as if she hadn't spoken, his voice curling over her skin, soothing and unsettling at the same time.

'What do you mean?' she said hoarsely.

He smiled. 'Isn't it obvious? We need to get married.'

The air was punched out of lungs. She stared at him in a daze, the beat of her heart suddenly deafeningly loud inside her head. She was mute with shock—not only at the audacity, the arrogance of his words, but at the heat building inside her.

How could she feel like that? Their marriage had been a disaster, and yet she could feel a part of herself responding with an eagerness that shocked her.

Ignoring the quivering sensation in her stomach, she forced herself to meet his gaze. 'That's not funny, Aristo.'

'It's not meant to be.' He looked at her, his gaze impassive. 'If I'm to be a permanent fixture in George's life then I need to be a permanent fixture in yours. Marriage is the simplest solution. We marry and George gets two parents and a stable, uncomplicated home life.'

She stared at him in disbelief. 'Is that what you think our marriage was like? Stable and uncomplicated?' She wanted to laugh, except that it wasn't even remotely amusing, just horribly familiar—for wasn't this exactly why they'd got divorced? Because Aristo had made assumptions without so much as considering her point of view or her feelings.

'I am not marrying you—*remarrying* you,' she corrected herself.

Tipping back his head, he stared down into her eyes. 'Why not? It's not something you haven't done before.'

She gaped at him. 'And it didn't work.' She enunciated each word with painstaking emphasis.

His dark gaze roamed so slowly over her face that she felt it like a caress.

'As I recall it worked very well.'

Her breath was trapped in her throat. 'I'm not talking about that,' she said quickly. 'I'm talking about everything else about our marriage. None of that worked.'

'Didn't work *last time*.' He dismissed her remark with a careless lift of his shoulders. 'But engaging with past mistakes is crucial to an improved performance, and this time we'll be operating from a position of experience, not ignorance.'

She felt her heart beat faster. He sounded as if he was presenting a business plan, not discussing getting married. But then, even before their marriage had ended work had already consumed his life to the exclusion of everything else—including her.

'This isn't some management strategy,' she said witheringly. 'This is my life, Aristo.'

His eyes didn't so much as flicker but she felt a sudden rise in tension.

'No, Teddie. This is our son's life. A son who doesn't know who I am. A son I've already let down. No child should feel like that.'

He stopped abruptly, his jaw tightening, and Teddie felt some of her anger deflate. There was something in his response that made her flinch inside, as though the words had been dragged out of him.

Aristo caught his breath. Remembering his own childhood, the constant nagging sense of not belonging, he felt suddenly sick. Whatever else happened, his son was going to feel wanted by *both* his parents.

'You haven't let him down.'

Teddie's voice jolted him back into real time and he gritted his teeth. She might have been his wife, but he'd never discussed his childhood with her. But the past was history. What mattered was George.

'I wasn't there—' He broke off and stared away, his face taut and set. 'All I want to do is make it up to him. And that is going to take more than a couple of trips to the swings.'

'You're right. I'm sorry.'

Teddie stared at his profile, her heartbeat rocking back and forth like a boat on a choppy sea. She could sense pain beneath his stilted words and she felt ashamed. Up until that moment she hadn't truly considered his feelings beyond shock and anger, and that had been unfair of her—for how would she be feeling right now if the situation was reversed?

'Maybe we should go away somewhere. That way you and George can spend time getting to know each other and we can start being open and honest with each other, because that's the only way we're going to make this work.'

Her words echoed inside her head, and for a moment she couldn't believe that they had actually come out of her mouth. But it was too late to take them back—and anyway, with a mixture of shock and relief she realised that she didn't actually want to. She needed to know now if Aristo was capable of being the father he claimed he wanted to be. Not in a few months, when it would destroy George if he left, just as she had been destroyed whenever her own father had disappeared from her life.

'Do you mean that?' His eyes were on hers, almost black, steady and unblinking.

'You want to get married again?' She phrased it as a question deliberately. 'Well, let's see if we can manage to spend a week together without wanting to kill each other.'

His eyes on her face were dark and intent. 'Or to tear each other's clothes off.'

Her pulse jolted forward, her body rippling into life as a wave of heat skimmed over her skin. For a moment she couldn't speak. Her brain seemed to have seized up and she stared at him in silence, stalling until finally she could lift her chin and meet his gaze.

'It would mean you taking time off work.' She tried and failed to keep the challenging note out of her voice.

There was a fraction of a pause. 'How does next week sound?' he said softly.

Her head snapped up. 'Next week?' The words made her feel giddy, but she could hardly back down now. 'That sounds fine. But won't it be a problem, going somewhere at such short notice?'

His eyes didn't leave hers. 'It won't be a problem at all. You see, I have an island—near Greece—and a plane to take us there.'

His mouth curled at the corners, his smile knocking the air out of her lungs.

'All you have to do is pack.'

CHAPTER FOUR

'LOOK, MOMMY, LOOK!'

Glancing up from the magazine lying open on her lap, Teddie smiled across the cabin to where George was waving a toy car at her.

'I can see, darling. Oh, wow!'

She made a suitably impressed face as he made the car fly up and then crash land on the headrest of his chair.

Over the top of her son's dark head her eyes met Aristo's, and quickly she looked away, not quite ready to share the moment with him.

She was still coming to terms with the fact that she was sitting on a private jet that was flying above the Atlantic Ocean. Obviously it had been her idea that they take a holiday. But, aside from her foreshortened honeymoon in St Bart's, she'd only ever been on day trips away. Now she was on her way to Greece! And not to the mainland but a private island—Aristo's island.

Out of the corner of her eye she could just see his smooth dark head, his black hair and light gold skin gleaming in the sunlit cabin. He was dressed casually, in jeans and some kind of fine-knit grey sweater, but he still exuded the same compelling air of authority and self-assurance.

She felt her heart beat faster. Everything was moving so fast. A part of her was glad about that, for if she'd had longer to think she would probably have been paralysed with indecision. And yet something about the speed with which everything had been set in motion made her feel uneasy.

Tucking a strand of dark hair behind her ear, she gazed meditatively out of the window at the horizon.

No doubt some of that feeling was down to being suddenly confronted by the true scale of Aristo's wealth. Four years ago his empire had been in its infancy—now, though, evidence of the Leonidas billions was visible everywhere, from his chauffeur-driven limousine to the powerfully built men in identical dark suits who had accompanied him onto the plane and were now seated at the other end of the cabin, studiously examining their phone screens.

She glanced over to where George and Aristo were playing with a sturdy wooden garage. It had been a gift from Aristo, supposedly to help occupy George during the long flight to Greece, but she had sensed that, more importantly for Aristo, it was an opportunity to connect with his son.

Her throat tightened. He could give George anything he wanted and, although she knew her son was happy and contented with his life, he was just as susceptible to the excitement of new toys or a promised trip on a speedboat as any other child. What would happen as he grew up? What if George chose to live with his glamorous, prosperous father?

One day he would have to choose because, whatever Aristo might think, she had no intention of marrying him again—ever.

Beneath the magazine, her hands balled into fists. *Don't go there*, she told herself, letting her long dark hair fall in front of her face. But it was too late. Like a dog proudly retrieving a stick for its owner, her brain had revealed the real reason why the haste and impulsiveness of this holiday had got under her skin.

She and Aristo had first got together after a particularly demanding week for her, and a charity dinner that she'd thought would never end. Aristo had been a guest at one of the tables.

Aged twenty-two, she'd had boyfriends, but never fallen in love, and she certainly hadn't been intending to fall in love that night. Even now she still wasn't quite sure how it had happened. Just that there had been something about the tilt of his head and the intensity of his gaze that had jolted her.

She'd picked him out to be her 'assistant', correctly identifying the card he'd chosen and then pickpocketing his watch.

Of course he'd had to come to the bar to retrieve

it, and then he'd stayed, and when the bar staff had started to clear up around them she had leaned forward and kissed him.

He'd kissed her back, and she'd taken his hand and led him upstairs to her room. They'd only just made it.

That first time had been fast, abandoned and fully clothed. The second time too. When finally they'd managed to undress, and were lying naked and spent in one another's arms, she had already been half in love with him.

To her surprise, they'd carried on seeing one another—meeting in hotels across America whenever his frequent trips abroad and her show schedule had permitted them to do so. And then, less than two months after they'd met, he'd surprised her in Las Vegas and said the words that had changed the course of her life.

'You can't keep on living out of a suitcase and I can't wait any longer—for you to be my wife.'

Given the example set by her parents, marriage had been the last thing on her mind, and yet she hadn't hesitated.

Her chest tightened. And look how that had turned out.

Two hours later George had finally succumbed to the excitement of the day, and lay sleeping across two seats, his car clutched tightly in his hand. Gently, she reached over and smoothed his dark hair away from his forehead, her heart contracting painfully.

He was so beautiful, so perfect, even given a mother's bias, and she loved him completely and with an intensity that made her feel both superhuman and yet horribly defenceless.

More importantly, he would be out for the count for at least an hour, so now was her chance to send Elliot the text she had promised him and have a little freshen up at the same time. In the small but luxurious bathroom, she splashed some water onto her face, retied her thick, dark hair and then, walking back to the jet's bedroom, she tapped out a short but reassuring message to Elliot and sent it before she could change her mind.

Whatever she wrote, she knew he was still going to worry, but all he needed to know right now was that she had everything under control. But as she sat down on the chair beside the bed, she felt a sliver of panic slip down her spine, and the cheery bravado of her text seemed suddenly a little premature, for standing in the doorway, two cups of coffee in his hands, was Aristo.

Her body tensed, her heart thudding against her ribs like a wrecking ball as he held them up by way of explanation.

'I thought you might like a coffee as we had such an early start.' His dark eyes rested on her face.

'You always used to hate getting up early.' There was a short, suspended silence.

Teddie felt her insides tighten and a prickling heat began to spread over her suddenly over-sensitised skin as she remembered exactly what it had felt like to wake in Aristo's arms.

Tuning out the memory of his hard golden body on hers, she lifted her chin. 'Now I have a three-year-old son,' she said coolly. Her breath fluttered in her chest as he put one of the cups on the cabinet beside her bed.

'How long does he normally sleep?'

'An hour and a half—maybe two today. He was so excited last night he couldn't settle.'

His mouth curved upwards into a slow, sweet smile that made it impossible for her to look away.

'I would have been just the same at his age. Will it mess up his routine?'

She shrugged. 'A little. He didn't eat much breakfast, so he's probably going to be really hungry.'

'We can have lunch when he wakes up.'

She felt a cool shiver shoot down her spine as Aristo dropped down into the bed opposite her. Clearing her throat, she nodded. 'That's a good idea.'

He hesitated. 'I don't know what he likes—I thought pasta, maybe, or pizza.'

He sounded conciliatory, disarmingly unsure,

and she felt some of her tension ebb. Maybe this was going to work—and she wanted it to, for George's sake at least.

Nodding, she gave him a stiff smile. 'Pasta or pizza will be fine. Although he's actually not fussy at all.'

She hesitated. Aristo had never been good at small talk or casual conversation—the silence between one of her questions and his answer had once stretched to twenty-three long drawn-out seconds—and the only times he'd ever unbent and seemed relaxed enough to chat had been during those long-distance phone calls late at night. But now, glancing up at his dark eyes, she saw that he was watching her without any hint of impatience.

'If he sees me eat something then he seems to think it's all right for him to eat too.'

'Smart boy,' Aristo said softly, and his eyes gleamed. 'Must take after his mother.'

It was the corniest of compliments, the sort of remark that didn't really warrant a response, but despite that she felt her cheeks grow warm beneath his dark, unblinking gaze.

'So,' he said softly into the taut silence, 'George seems to be getting used to me.'

'He likes you.' She raised an eyebrow. 'But I'm sure that will change when he gets to know you better.'

He stared at her steadily. 'We can make this work, Teddie.'

'I'm sure we can,' she said evenly. 'It would be pretty difficult not to. I mean, it's a holiday on a Greek island.'

She picked up her coffee, wishing that the cup was large enough for her to climb inside and hide from his dark, level gaze.

'I wasn't talking about the holiday.'

His expression was gently mocking, and she felt her heart start to beat faster. She'd known, of course, that he wasn't talking about the holiday, but she'd been hoping to keep away from that particular subject. But if he wanted to talk about it, then, fine.

She breathed out slowly. 'I know that you want this week to be some kind of first step towards me changing my mind about marrying you, but that's not why I'm here,' she said firmly. 'I'm happy for you to be in George's life but, honestly, something truly incredible—unimaginable, in fact—would have to happen for me to want to be your wife again. So could we drop this, please?'

He didn't respond, but she could sense a shift in his mood, sense something slipping away.

'What alternative is there?'

The bluntness of his question caught her off-guard. 'I don't know. The usual options, I suppose. Shared custody. Holidays and weekends— What?'

He was shaking his head and she felt a flare of anger.

'We don't work as a couple. You know that.' She stared at him, a beat of frustration pulsing in her chest. 'So stop pretending that marriage is an option.'

His eyes hardened. 'Only if you stop being so stubborn and try see it from my perspective for once.'

She glared at him. 'We should never have got married in the first place, so why would I ever want to do it again? In fact—' she took a breath, and straightened her shoulders '—why would *you* ever want to do it again? No, please, Aristo—just explain to me why you'd want to do something that made you so unhappy and angry.'

Aristo stared back at her in silence, his heart pressing against his ribs, caught off-guard by this unexpected and startling assessment of their relationship. 'I wasn't angry,' he said finally. 'I was confused because you were so dissatisfied.'

He watched her shake her head.

'Angry…dissatisfied…what does it matter anyway? We were both unhappy, so why would we do it again?'

His chest tightened and he felt a rush of anger and frustration with her for pushing—and with himself for thinking she would understand.

Before he could stop himself—before he even

fully understood what he was about to do—he said, 'Because I know what it feels like when your father turns into a stranger.'

Listening to his words bounce around the quiet cabin, he felt his back tense and a hum of panic start to sing inside his head. What was he thinking? He'd never discussed his past with anyone. *Ever.* So why choose this of all moments to start spilling his guts about his childhood?

There was a tiny, sharp silence, like a splinter of ice, and through his dark lashes he could sense her confusion.

'I thought you inherited the business from your father?' she said slowly.

'I did.' His voice sounded sharp, too sharp, but he didn't care. He just stared past her, his back aching.

'So, when did he—?' She stopped, frowned, and then tried again. 'How is he a stranger? Did something happen? Did you argue?'

Looking up, he found her watching him, and for a second he felt light-headed, almost as though he was floating. He was shocked to see not just confusion in her wide green eyes, but genuine concern too.

He hesitated. Now the words were out, he wasn't sure what to say next, or what Teddie was expecting to hear. The truth, probably. But the truth was way more complex and revealing than he could bring himself to admit, and to Teddie most of all.

'No, we didn't argue,' he said finally, with a firmness that he hoped would dissuade further discussion. 'Just forget about it.'

Teddie stared at him uncertainly, her mind doing cartwheels. She felt as if she had stepped through a wardrobe into a strange new country. This was not the Aristo she knew.

But then what did she really know about her aloof, uncompromising ex-husband? Their relationship hadn't been based on mutual interests or friends. The first few weeks of their affair had been carried out long-distance, and those long phone calls that she'd so come to enjoy had been about the present—his latest deal, her hotel room—and how much they missed one another, how much they missed making love.

They had never once been about their pasts or their families. She hadn't asked and he hadn't volunteered—and in a way hadn't she been grateful? In fact, she might even have encouraged it. She'd certainly discouraged speculation about her background and awkward conversations about her own parents. Maybe a part of her had even found it romantic that he'd wanted it to be just about the two of them.

Now, though, it seemed his reticence had been based not on romance, or the speed of their relationship, but something more fundamental.

Watching Aristo rub the corners of his eyes, Teddie felt a sudden ache of misery, for it was exactly the same gesture that George made when he was tired or upset. And suddenly she knew why he was so insistent that they remarry.

'Did they get divorced?'

The question sounded ludicrously, simplistically trite, but she didn't know how else to begin—how else to get past that shuttered expression on his face. All she knew was that it had taken six months of a failed marriage and four years of separation to get to this moment, and she wasn't about to back off now. Even if that meant nudging at the boundaries of what he clearly considered off-limits.

Finally, he nodded. 'When I was six.'

His face was carefully blank, but she could hear the strain in his voice. Once again she had that sense of words being forcibly pulled out of him, and she knew that he'd never told this story before.

'That's young,' she said quietly.

He stayed silent for so long that she thought perhaps he hadn't heard her speak, and then, breathing out slowly, he nodded. 'My mother got remarried to this English lord, so they sold the house in Greece and I moved to England with my mother, to live with her and my stepfather, Peter.'

Her mind rewound through her rudimentary knowledge of Aristo's life. How had she not known about this? She'd been married to this man, loved him and had her heart shattered by him, and yet she knew so little. But she was starting to understand now why he was being so insistent about them remarrying. The adults in his life had made decisions based on their needs, not their son's, and in his eyes it must seem as if she had done the same with George.

'And what about your father?'

His shoulders stiffened, as though bracing against some hidden pain. 'He moved to America.'

She stared at him in silence, wanting to pull him close and hold him closer, to do anything that might ease the bruise in his voice and the taut set to his mouth. Except she was too afraid to move, afraid to do anything that might make him stop speaking.

'How did you get to see him?' she asked softly.

His shoulders shifted almost imperceptibly again. 'With difficulty. After we moved I was sent to boarding school, so there was only really the holidays, but by then my mother had a new baby— my half-brother, Oliver—and my father had re-married so everyone had got other stuff going on.'

Everyone but me.

She heard the unspoken end to his sentence, could picture the lonely, confused six-year-old Aristo, who would have looked a lot like their own son.

A muscle flickered in his jaw. 'After a couple of years it sort of petered out to one visit a year, and then it just stopped. He used to call occasionally—he still does.' He looked away, out of the window. 'But we don't really have anything to say to one another.'

He hesitated.

'I dream about him sometimes. And the crazy thing is that in my dreams he wants to talk to me.' His mouth twisted. 'Probably the longest conversation I actually had with him was when he signed the business over to me.'

He fell silent and, her heart thudding, she tried to think of something positive to say. 'But he did give you the business. Maybe that was his way of trying to show how much he cared.'

'I hope not.' Aristo turned to meet her eyes, his mouth twisting—part grimace, not quite a smile. 'Given that he was on the verge of filing for bankruptcy. The company was a wreck and he was up to his neck in debt—he hadn't even been paying the staff properly.'

'And *you* turned it around,' she said quickly. 'He could have just walked away, but I think he had faith in you. He knew you'd do the right thing.'

Her chin jerked upwards, and he watched her eyes narrow, the luminous green like twin lightning flashes.

'You've worked so hard and built something incredible. I know he must be proud of you.'

Teddie stared at him, her heart thudding so hard that it hurt. At the time of their marriage she'd hated his business, resented all the hours he'd spent working late into the night. But this wasn't about her or her feelings, it was about Aristo—about a little boy who had grown up needing to prove himself worthy of his inheritance.

She felt a little sick.

Was it any surprise that he was so intently focused on his career? Or that success mattered so much to him. He clearly wanted to prove himself, and felt responsible for saving his father's business—that would have had a huge impact on his character.

She felt his gaze, and looking up found her eyes locked with his.

'I don't expect you to understand how I'm feeling,' he said eventually. 'All I want to do is be the best father I can possibly be. Does that make sense?'

She bit her lip.

The best father I can possibly be.

His words replayed inside her head, alongside a memory of herself on the night that George had been born. Alone in her hospital room, holding her tiny new son, seeing his dark trusting eyes fixed on her face, she'd made a promise to him. A promise to be the best mother she could possibly be.

'I do understand.'

She was surprised by how calm and even her voice sounded. More surprised still that she was admitting that fact to Aristo. But how could she not tell him the truth when he had just shared what was clearly such a painfully raw memory of his own?

'I felt exactly the same way when I was pregnant. And it's what I wake up feeling most mornings.'

Hearing the edge in her voice, Aristo felt something unspool inside his chest. She looked uncertain. Teddie—who could stand in front of an audience and pluck the right card out of a deck without so much as blinking. He hated knowing that she had felt like that, that she still did.

When he was sure his voice was under control he said carefully, 'Why do you feel like that?'

It seemed irrational: to him, Teddie seemed such a loving, devoted mother.

She shrugged. 'My mom struggled. And my dad was...'

She hesitated and he waited, watching her decide whether to continue, praying that she would.

Finally, she cleared her throat. 'My dad was always away on business.' The euphemism slipped off her tongue effortlessly, before she was even aware that she was using it. 'And my mom couldn't really cope on her own. She started drinking, and then she had an accident. She fell down a staircase and smashed two of her vertebrae. She was in a lot of pain and they put her on medication.

She got addicted to it, and that's when she really went downhill.'

Even to her—someone who was familiar with the whole squalid mess that had been her childhood—it sounded appalling. Not just tragic, but pitiful.

Breathing out unsteadily, she gave him a tiny twist of a smile. 'After that she really couldn't cope at all—not with her job, or the apartment, or me… with anything, really.'

He frowned, trying to follow the thread of her logic, aching to go over and put his arms around her and hold her close. 'And you thought you would be like her?' he asked, careful to phrase it as a question, not a statement of fact.

She pulled a face. 'Not just her—it runs in the family. My mum was brought up by foster parents because *her* mother couldn't cope with her.' Her lips tightened.

'But you do cope,' he said gently and, reaching out, he took her hand and squeezed it. 'With everything. You run your own business. You have a lovely apartment and you're a wonderful mother.'

Abruptly she pulled her hand away. 'You don't have to say those things,' she said crossly, trying her hardest to ignore the way her pulse was darting crazily beneath her skin like a startled fish. 'You can't flatter me into marrying you, Aristo.'

Dark eyes gleaming, he leaned forward and pulled her reluctantly onto the bed beside him.

'Apparently not. And I know I don't have to say those things,' he added, his thumbs moving in slow, gentle strokes over her skin. 'I said them because I should have said them before and I didn't. I'm saying them because they're true.'

Releasing her, he reached up, his palms sliding through her hair, his fingers caressing then tightening, capturing her, his touch both firm and tender.

'So could I please just be allowed to say them? To you? Here? Now?'

Teddie blinked and, lifting her hand, touched his face, unable to resist stroking the smooth curving contour of his chin and cheekbone. She felt her fingertips tingling as they trailed over the graze of stubble already darkening his jawline.

Somewhere in the deepest part of her mind a drum had started to throb. She wanted to pull away from him—only not nearly as much as she wanted to feel his skin against hers, to lean into his solid shoulder.

'I suppose so.'

His thumb was stroking her cheek now. It was tracing the line of her lips and she could feel her brain slowing in time to her pulse.

'Aristo...' she said softly. The nearness of his drowsy, dark gaze nearly overwhelmed her.

'Yes, Teddie?'

'I don't think we should be doing this.'

The corners of his mouth—his beautiful mouth that was so temptingly close to hers—curved up into a tiny smile. 'We're not doing this because we should,' he said softly. 'We're doing this because we want to do it.'

Her stomach flipped over and she stilled, too scared to move, for she knew what would happen if she did. She knew exactly how her body would melt into his and just how intensely, blissfully good it would be.

But if she gave in and followed that beating drum of desire where would it lead? She might consider herself to be sexually carefree and independent, and maybe with any other man she could be that woman. But not with Aristo. Sharing her body with him would be fierce and intimate and all-consuming. She knew she would *feel* something—and that would make her vulnerable, and she couldn't be vulnerable around this man. Or at least not any more vulnerable than she already was.

And, whatever Aristo might argue to the contrary, when he talked about wanting to marry her again she knew deep down that what he was really thinking about was sex. Only, no matter how sublime it was, there was more to a relationship than sex—as their previous marriage had already painfully proved. She wouldn't—she couldn't—go there again.

Yes, she wanted to touch him, and she wanted him to hold her, and she was fighting herself, torn between wanting to believe that they could try again and knowing it was an impossibility. Maybe in another life, if the timing had been different...

But Aristo was already her first love, her ex-husband and the father of her child. Did she really need to add another layer of complication to what was already a complex and conflicted relationship? And besides, she should be looking forward, not back, and that meant keeping the past where it belonged.

'I know,' she said quietly. 'But this isn't about what you and I *want* any more. It's about being honest and open.'

His eyes moved over her face. 'So tell me, honestly, that you don't want me.'

He was so close she could see herself reflected in the dark pools of his eyes, and it took every atom of will in her body to resist the tractor beam of his gaze and her own longing.

'I can't. But I also know that I can't have everything I want. Maybe I thought I could once, but not any more.'

As the words left her mouth she knew that they were just that—words—and that if he chose to challenge her or, worse, if he leaned forward and kissed her, she would be lost.

She stared at him, mute, transfixed, mind and body wavering between desire and panic.

But he didn't lean forward.

Instead, his dark eyes calm, his expression un-fathomable, he gently ran a finger down the side of her face and then, standing up, walked slowly across the cabin. As the door closed she breathed out unsteadily, searching inwardly for the relief she'd expected to feel.

But it wasn't there. Instead she had never felt lonelier, or more confused.

CHAPTER FIVE

STEPPING OUT OF the shower, Aristo reached for a towel and rubbed it briefly over his lean, muscular body. He smoothed his damp hair against his skull and, still naked, stepped into his dressing room. Stopping in front of the shelves, he let his dark eyes scan their colour-coded contents momentarily, before picking out a pair of dark blue swim shorts and a lighter blue T-shirt.

He sighed. If only the rest of his life could be as organised and straightforward.

Sliding his watch over his knuckles, he glanced down at the time and frowned. It was early—far too early for anyone else on the island to be awake. But although it was the first day of his holiday his body still insisted on acting as though it was just another day at the office.

Actually, not *all* of his body, he thought grimly. Twelve hours on a plane with Teddie had left him aching with a sexual frustration that made not just sleep but relaxing almost impossible.

He grimaced. Only, in comparison to what was going on inside his head, the discomfort in his groin seemed completely inconsequential.

His heart began to beat unsteadily.

Had he really told Teddie all that stuff about his father? He could hardly believe it.

He'd spent most of his adolescence and adult life suppressing that hurt and disappointment, building barriers between himself and the world, and especially between himself and his wife. Ordinarily he found it easy to deter personal questions. But yesterday Teddie had refused to take no for an answer. Instead she had waited, and listened, and coaxed the truth out of him.

Not the whole truth, of course—he would never be ready to share that with anyone—just the reason why he was so determined to remarry her.

It had been hard enough to reveal even that much, for it had been the first time he'd ever really tried to untangle the mess of emotions he felt for his father. The first time he'd spoken out loud about Apostolos's indifference and almost total absence from his life.

It had been a rare loss of self-control—one that he still couldn't fully explain. But Teddie had been, and was still, the only person who could get under his skin and make him see fifty shades of red. She alone had overridden all his carefully placed defences, and it wasn't the first time it had happened. Despite her being the wrong woman in the wrong place at the wrong time, he'd not only led her to his bedroom but up the aisle.

His mind took him back to the moment when

he'd first become aware of the existence of Teddie Taylor at the opening of his first major project—the Rocky Creek Ranch. It had been a vision nearly two years in the making: a luxury resort offering all-American activities on a three-thousand-acre mountain playground.

He'd wanted his mother, Helena, to be there, but inevitably—and despite his reminding her frequently about the date—there had been a clash. His half-brother, Oliver, had been playing in some polo match, so his mother had missed what had been up until then the most important moment in his career.

He'd almost not gone to the opening. But as usual business had overridden emotion and he'd bitten down on his disappointment and joined the specially selected guests to watch the evening's cabaret.

He wasn't entirely sure when Teddie had stopped being just the entertainment. He'd barely registered the other acts and, although he'd thought her beautiful, she was not his usual type. Only, at some point, as she had effortlessly shuffled and cut the cards in front of her captive audience, he'd been unable to look away—and, despite believing himself indifferent to magic, he'd found himself falling under her spell.

Catching a glimpse of green eyes the colour of unripe olives, he'd willed her to look at him, and just as though he'd waved a magic wand she picked him out from the crowd. Even now he could still remember the jolt of electricity as their hands had touched, but at the end of the performance she'd turned away to mingle with the other guests.

Only, of course that hadn't really been the end of her performance.

She'd been waiting for him in the bar.

With the watch she'd removed from his wrist.

Seven weeks later they had been married, and six months after that they'd been divorced.

Angry and hurt, he'd cast her as the villain, believing that she'd seen him as a warm-up act—a means to gain access to the kind of society where there would be rich pickings for a beautiful, smart and sexy woman like Teddie Taylor.

Now, with hindsight, he could see that it had been easy to persuade himself that those were the cold, hard facts, for there had been a deeper anger there. An anger with himself. Anger because he'd allowed himself to be drawn to a woman like her after all he'd been through and seen.

He frowned. Four years ago it had all seemed so simple. He'd thought he understood Teddie completely.

Now, though, it was clear that he'd never really understood her at all. Worse, his previous assessment of her seemed to bear no relation to the woman who had been so worried about him on the plane. Or to the woman who had financially supported herself and their child on her own.

A light breeze ruffled the white muslin curtains and he turned towards the window, his eyes lingering on the calm blue sea that stretched out to the horizon in every direction. Had the single-mindedness that had always been his greatest strength actually been a weakness? Had he put two and two together and made minus four?

Frowning again, he stepped towards the window, pondering how that could be the case.

Although he'd condemned her as shallow and grasping when they'd split up, he couldn't ignore the facts, and the truth was that Teddie had neither challenged the modest settlement she'd received at the time of their divorce—a settlement which had obviously not included raising George—or pursued him for more money.

In fact she had successfully supported both herself and their son *without him*, and reluctantly, he found himself contemplating the astonishing possibility that he might actually have misjudged Teddie. That maybe he'd cut and pasted his parents' mismatched and unhappy relationship onto his own marriage, making the facts fit the theory.

But what *were* the facts about his ex-wife? What did he really know about Teddie?

He breathed out slowly and started walking towards the door. Judging by that conversation on the plane, not as much as he'd thought he did. Or as much as he should.

Teddie had been his wife. He might not remember his vows word for word—there had been too much adrenaline in his blood, and a sense of standing on the edge of a cliff—but surely her husband should have been the person who knew her best.

Thinking about her baffling remarks on the plane, he felt his shoulders tense.

Yesterday she'd as good as admitted that she wanted him—why, then, had she held back? And what had she meant by telling him that she couldn't have everything she wanted?

He felt his heartbeat slow.

In principle, this holiday was supposed to be all about getting to know his son, but clearly he needed to get to know his ex-wife as well. In fact it wasn't just a need—he *wanted* to get to know Teddie, to get close to her.

His legs stopped moving, and something exploded inside his chest like a firecracker as he realised that he wasn't just talking about her body. No, what really fascinated him about his beautiful, infuriating, mysterious ex-wife was her mind.

His heartbeat doubled, a flare of excitement catching him off-guard.

Last time they hadn't got to know each other as people. It hadn't been that kind of relationship, or even any relationship really—just desire, raw and intoxicating as moonshine.

Marriage had been the furthest thought from his mind. Even now he didn't understand why he'd done it. Watching his father be taken for a fool should have been warning enough to steer clear of matrimony, but Teddie had slipped past his defences.

And now she was the mother of his child, and the logical and necessary consequence of that fact was that they should remarry, for it was his job to take care of his child and the mother of his child.

Only, this time it would be different—more like a business deal. There would be no messy emotions or expectations. He would set the boundaries, and there would be no overstepping them, and then he would have it all—a global business empire, a beautiful wife and a son.

All he needed to do now was convince Teddie to give him a second chance.

He blew out a breath. Judging by her continued resistance to even the possibility of renewing their relationship, that was going to be something of a challenge—particularly as he didn't know where or how to start.

But so what if he didn't have all the answers? What he did know for certain was that as of now he was going to do whatever it took to find out what made Teddie Taylor tick.

And, feeling calmer than he had in days, he started walking towards the door again.

'Wait a minute, George.' Turning her son gently to face her, Teddie rubbed sunscreen into the soft skin of his arms, marvelling as she did every morning that she'd had anything to do with producing this beautiful little human.

His small face was turned up towards hers, the dark eyes watching her trustingly, and she felt her heart contract not only with love but at the knowledge that she had never felt as her son did. He had been raised to feel secure in a world where he was loved and protected. Whereas she had known nothing but a life spent in flux, with parents who had been absent either in body or mind.

She thought about herself at the same age. Of her mother, drifting through the house in a haze of painkillers, barely registering her small daughter. And then she thought of herself a few years later, at school, when her constant fear had been that her mother's fixed smile and narcotised stare would be obvious to others.

It had felt like a dead weight inside her chest, a burden without respite—for of course her father had been away, his wife and daughter no match for whatever get-rich-quick scheme he had been chasing.

'Mommy, are we going in the pool now?'

'We are.' She smiled down at her son's excited face. He had been talking about nothing else since he'd woken up. 'Just let me find your hat.'

He frowned. 'I don't want to wear it.'

'I know,' she said calmly. 'But it's hot outside and you need to protect your head. I'm going to be wearing *my* hat.' She pointed to the oversized straw hat she'd seen and then impulse-bought in a shop on her way home from work.

George stared up at her. 'Does Aristo have a hat too?'

Her smile stiffened. 'I don't know. He might do.'

Looking down into her son's dark eyes—eyes that so resembled his father's—Teddie felt her stomach flip over, as it did every single time George mentioned Aristo's name.

But it was a small price to pay for being permitted into paradise, she thought, closing the tube of sunscreen as she glanced at the view from her window. The island was beautiful. Although just an hour by motorboat from the mainland, it felt otherworldly, mythical.

It was a wisp of land with bleached sandy beaches and coves, and luminous turquoise water so clear you could see every ripple on the seabed. The villa itself looked like something you might read about in one of those glossy lifestyle magazines, dazzling white beneath the fierce sunlight. There were views everywhere of the sky and sea, and occasional glimpses of the elliptically-shaped pool—blue on blue on blue. And if all that wasn't enough, there was a garden filled with fruit trees and the drowsy hum of bees.

It was untouched and timeless, and in another life she could have imagined switching off and losing herself in its raw, unpolished beauty and sage-scented air.

But, despite the sun-drenched peace of her surroundings, and her own composed appearance, she felt anything but calm.

She'd woken early from a dream—something familiar but imprecise—and it had taken her a wild moment to remember where she was. Lying back against the pressed white linen pillowcase, she had steadied her breathing. Her restless mind, though, had proved harder to soothe.

Ever since she'd walked out of Aristo's office she'd been trying to come to terms with everything that had happened and how she was feeling about it.

Or, more specifically, how she was feeling about the man who had just barged back into her life—for, as much as she'd have liked to pretend otherwise, it wasn't this heavenly island that was dominating her thoughts but her ex-husband.

Perhaps, though, that was progress of a sort. For at least now she could admit, even if only to herself, that Aristo had always been in the background of her life.

Of course she'd wanted to forget him. She'd tried hard to make it appear as though he'd never existed. And outwardly she'd succeeded. She had a job and friends and an apartment, and they were all separate from her life with Aristo. But she could see now that her unresolved feelings for him had continued to influence the way she lived. Why else had she kept every other man except Elliot at a distance? Even the sweet single dads she met at nursery.

Her fingers tightened around the sunscreen.

Not that it would have made any difference if she'd welcomed them with open arms. What man was ever going to be able to match Aristotle Leonidas? He had shaped her life and he was an impossible act to follow on so many levels—not just in terms of his wealth or even his astonishing beauty. There was an elusive quality to him that fascinated her. He was like a mirage that shimmered in the distance, hazy and tantalising, always just out of reach, slipping between her fingers like smoke.

Her heart began to beat faster.

Except yesterday, when out of nowhere he'd suddenly unbent, opening up to her about his childhood in a way that she would never have imagined possible. It had been a brief glimpse into what had made him the man he was, but also a fairly damning reflection on their marriage—for how could she have known so little about the man who had been her lover and her husband?

It wasn't all her fault, though, she thought defensively. Aristo had been as reluctant to discuss his past as she had, and a part of her couldn't help but wonder if it wouldn't have been a lot easier if they'd had that conversation four years ago,

Instead, though, he had stonewalled her, and she'd run away.

And if she hadn't been marooned on an island on the other side of the world that was what she should be doing now—beating a dignified but hasty retreat from his unsettling, dangerously tempting presence.

Picking up George's hat, she shivered at the memory of how close she'd come to giving in to that temptation. She was just so vulnerable where Aristo was concerned… Only, it went deeper than that. Her need to exonerate and turn a blind eye was rooted in a childhood spent craving and competing for her father's attention.

It had been the pattern of her early life: Wyatt's intermittent absences followed by his inevitable reappearance. No matter how unhappy and angry she'd been, every time he'd come back she'd let herself believe his promises, allowed herself to care. And every time he had left she had felt more worthless than the time before.

And that was why she wasn't going to fall into the same pattern with Aristo.

No matter how sexy or charming he was, one shared confidence couldn't change the facts. It was too little, too late. They didn't trust each other, and that was why their marriage had failed—why she couldn't give in to the sexual pull between them now.

Making love with Aristo again would undoubtedly be unforgettable, but she knew from experience that the people she cared about found it exceptionally easy to forget *her*.

That episode in the plane had hinted at what would happen if she gave in, how quickly everything would start to unravel...

She breathed out slowly. Was that true, or was she overreacting? After all, what was really so wrong about two people who had once shared a unique and powerful chemistry getting together again? Plenty of people did it: Elliot for one.

Only, this was different. There was George to consider, so there would be no way out...nowhere to run.

Her mouth was suddenly dry and she felt a rushing panic, like a stone dropping into the darkness. And besides, this wasn't some game of spin the bottle—and Aristo wasn't some old flame she could casually reignite.

He was a forest fire.

One touch was all it had taken to awaken her body from hibernation. One more touch and she would be lost. And next time she felt like giving in to the heat of his body and the strength of his shoulders she needed to remember that.

Outside on the terrace, George instantly tugged his hand free and scampered towards Aristo. She followed him reluctantly, suddenly conscious of the fact that both she and Aristo were semi-naked, and wishing that she'd packed a one-piece as well as her bikinis.

George was gazing up at his father. 'I want you to take me swimming.'

Aristo laughed. 'So let's go swimming.' He hesitated. 'Is that all right?' Glancing over, he stared at her questioningly, and she almost burst out laughing, for his expression so closely mirrored their small son's.

Nodding, she turned towards George. 'Yes, but you have to do what Aristo tells you.'

She felt it on her skin before she saw it: the slow upturn of his mouth, the teasing glitter in his dark eyes.

'Does that go for you too?' he asked softly.

Her heartbeat faltered. Somewhere beyond her suddenly blurred vision she heard the faint splash of waves as a pulse of excitement began beating beneath her skin. For a sharp, dizzying second they stared at each other, and then, glancing pointedly back at George, she smiled.

'I'm going to read my book, darling. I'll be just over here, okay?'

Ignoring the amusement in Aristo's eyes, she quickly sat down on one of the loungers that had been arranged temptingly around the pool. Unwrapping her sarong, she stretched out her legs and glanced over to where Aristo had been sitting. Instantly her mood shifted. A mass of documents were spread out over the table and beside them, open in the sunshine, was his laptop.

Seriously? Had he really brought work with him?

Her eyes narrowed. But when had Aristo ever put work anywhere but first on his agenda? She thought back to the long, empty evenings she'd spent alone in their beautiful cavernous apartment, feeling that same sense of failure and fear that she was not enough to deserve anyone's unswerving attention.

Fleetingly she considered saying something— but it was only the first day of their holiday, so maybe she should give him the benefit of the doubt. After all, he had walked away from his office at a moment's notice, and that would have meant unpicking a full diary of meetings and appointments.

Out of the corner of her eye she caught a glimpse of hard, primed muscle, and instantly a heat that had nothing to do with the Mediterranean sun spread slowly over her skin.

Picking up her book, she opened it at random, irritated that, even when faced with evidence of his continuing obsession with work, her body still seemed stubbornly and irrationally determined to ignore the bad in favour of the good.

There was a loud splash, and automatically her eyes darted over to where the 'good' was unapologetically on display. In the shallow end of the pool Aristo was raising George out of the water on his shoulders, droplets of water trickling down the muscles of his arms and chest, and in the dazzling golden light he looked shockingly beautiful.

She gritted her teeth. Why couldn't he own a ski lodge? Some snowbound chalet where quilted jackets and chunky jumpers were practically mandatory? she thought, her heart thumping as Aristo stood up and began to walk out of the water, the wet fabric of his shorts clinging to the blatantly masculine outline of his body.

Fully clothed and in a crowded hotel he had been hard to ignore, but half naked on a private island he was almost impossible to resist.

As though reading her mind, Aristo chose that particular moment to look over at her, and she felt a cool tingle run down her spine as his dark eyes drifted over her face, homing in on her mouth in a way that emptied the breath from her lungs.

She wanted to look away, but forced herself to meet his eyes—and then immediately wished she hadn't as his piercing gaze dropped to the pulse beating agitatedly at the base of her throat, then lower still to the curve of her breasts beneath the peach-coloured bikini.

'Look at me, Mommy! Look!' George waved his hands excitedly.

'Don't worry, George,' Aristo said softly, his dark eyes gleaming. 'Mommy's looking.'

Her skin was prickling as, still carrying their giggling son, he walked slowly towards her. Depositing George onto his feet, he dropped down lightly onto the lounger beside her, his cool, damp body sending a jolt over her skin like sheet lightning.

'Here.' Grabbing a towel, she unceremoniously pushed it into his hands. 'Why don't you dry off?'

'I thought you might like to take a dip with me.'

His voice was cool and controlled, but the taunting expression in his eyes made her breath catch in her throat.

'Or are you scared of getting out of your depth?'

Their gazes locked and she wondered how it was possible that one little sentence could make her feel her so naked and exposed.

She tried to think of something smart to say, but she was struggling to control her voice. 'No, of course I'm not scared.' She glared at him.

His eyes hadn't left her face. 'Did you hear that,

George?' He glanced slyly over at his son. 'Mommy's going to come swimming with us.'

'I didn't say that—' But as George began jumping up and down, she gave up. She held up her hands. 'Okay, okay—I'll go swimming. But later.'

Her face grew warm as she felt his dark eyes slowly inspect her, his narrowed gaze rolling over each of her ribs like a car over speed bumps.

'That colour really suits you,' he said softly.

Leaning forward, he tipped her book upwards to glance at the cover and she felt his thigh press against hers. Her mouth suddenly dry, she stared across at him.

'Thank you.' She felt her lips move, heard her voice, but none of it felt real. Nothing felt real, in fact, except the hard length of his leg.

'Mommy? Please may I have a juice?'

Turning towards her son, she nodded. 'Of course, darling.'

'I'll take him.' Aristo stood up, and she clenched her muscles against the sudden, almost brutal feeling of loss as she watched her son trotting happily beside her ex-husband towards the villa.

Later, she joined them in the pool, and then she dozed in the sunshine while Aristo taught George to do a kneeling dive.

It felt strange, watching the two of them. In fact she felt the tiniest bit jealous of her son's fascination with Aristo, for up until now it had always been just the two of them. Mainly, though, she was stunned but happy at how quickly and effortlessly they had bonded, and at the fact that Aristo seemed as enchanted by George as she was.

A knot began to form in her stomach. It had caught her off-guard, Aristo being so gentle and patient with his son. Growing up, that had been all she'd ever wanted from her own father—to be more than the fleeting focus of his wandering attention. And the blossoming relationship between Aristo and George was not merely a reminder of what she'd missed out on growing up, it also confirmed what she'd already subconsciously accepted—that there was no going back. They were going to have to tell George the truth.

Gazing down at the open but unread page of her book, Teddie felt a flicker of panic. Not about her son's likely reaction to the news, but about what would happen when they left the island and returned to normal life.

Aristo might appear to be fully focused on George right now, but this was the honeymoon period, and she knew how swiftly and devastatingly things could change. Back in New York, her son would no longer be the only item on Aristo's agenda. He was going to have to compete for his father's time against the allure and challenge of work.

The tension in her chest wound tighter and

tighter and she gripped the edges of the book, re-membering how glorious it had been to feel the warmth of his gaze. And how cold it had felt when she'd been pushed into the shadows.

But it was too late to worry about that now. George wasn't going to stay as a three-year-old for ever, and sooner or later he was going to want to know who his father was. And—as she'd already discovered—there was never a right time to tell the truth.

'I thought we might eat together later tonight. Just the two of us.'

Aristo's voice cut into her thoughts and her chin jerked up. They were lazing by the pool beneath a gleaming white canvas canopy. His gaze was steady, his voice measured.

'We need to talk,' he said quietly. 'And, much as I love having our son around, it'll be easier to do that when he's not there.'

She knew her face had stilled. Her heart had stilled too, at the thought of spending an evening alone with him. But, ignoring the panicky drum-ming of her heart, she nodded. 'I agree.'

And then, before her face could betray her, she lowered the brim of her hat and leaned back against the sun lounger.

Three hours later, the heat of the day was starting to drop and a faint breeze was riffling the glassy surface of the pool.

Glancing down at her cup of coffee, Teddie felt her spine tense. The meal would soon be over, but she still hadn't managed to say even one word of what was whirling inside her head.

Looking up, she felt her heart drop forward like a rollercoaster. Aristo was watching her, his gaze so calm and knowing that she felt as if she'd been caught with her hand in his jacket. Except he wasn't wearing a jacket.

Just a washed-out black Henley and a pair of cream linen trousers.

'You're quiet,' he said softly.

'Am I?' She felt her cheeks flush, hearing the nervousness in her voice.

'Yes, unnervingly so.' His eyes looked directly into hers and she suddenly wished that it was whisky, not coffee that she was drinking.

She frowned. 'I'm just thinking…'

'Whoa! I wasn't getting at you. I don't want to fight.'

He held up his napkin and waved it in a gesture of surrender, but she barely noticed; she was too busy following the lazy curve of his smile.

Her own smile was instant, instinctive, unstoppable. 'I'm not looking for a fight either…' She hesitated. 'I was just thinking about us, and George, and…'

He sat watching her, waiting, and she looked away, fearful of what she would see in his eyes.

'And… Well, I think we should tell him tomorrow that you're his father.'

There was a stretch of silence.

Aristo studied her face.

Caught between the flickering nightlights and the darkness she looked tense, wary, apprehensive and he could sense the effort her words had taken.

Of course, logically, now he and George had met, it was inevitable that they should tell him the truth, and it was what he wanted—or at least a part of what he wanted. But, as much as he wanted to acknowledge his son as his own, these last few days had taught him that the decision needed to come from Teddie.

And now it had.

He exhaled slowly, relief vying with satisfaction. It wasn't quite the hand of friendship, but it was a start.

His eyes wandered idly over the simple yellow dress she was wearing, lingering on the upward curve of her breasts. And anyway, he wanted Teddie to be a whole lot more than just a friend.

'Are you sure?' He spoke carefully. 'We can wait. *I* can wait.'

He was rapidly becoming an expert in waiting. Shifting against the ache in his groin, he gritted his teeth and glanced away to the white line of slow-moving surf down on the beach.

Teddie felt her heart jump against her ribs. Incredibly, Aristo was giving her a choice, but to her surprise she realised that now was the right time.

'I'm sure.'

And once they did then there really would be no going back.

She felt a spasm of panic, needle-sharp, like a blade beneath her ribs. Was she doing the right thing? Or had she just doomed her son to the same fate that she'd endured? A childhood marked with uncertainty and self-doubt, with a father who would cloak his absences beneath the virtuous task of supporting his family.

'He needs to know.' Hearing the words out loud, she felt tears coming. Quickly she bolstered her panic. 'But I need to know that you understand what this means.'

He frowned. 'If I didn't I wouldn't be here.'

Pushing back her chair, she stood up unsteadily. 'So this is all about you, is it?'

'That's not what I'm saying.'

He was standing now too.

'That's what it sounded like.'

She heard him inhale and her anger shifted to guilt. It wasn't fair to twist his words when she wasn't being honest about her own feelings.

'I just mean that being a father is a lifetime commitment.'

His face hardened. 'I'd like to say that's not something I'm going to forget but, given my own childhood, I can't. All I can say is that I am going to be there for George—for you.'

Teddie fought the beating of her heart. He was saying all the right things and she wanted to believe him—only believing him set off in her a whole new spiral of half-thought-out fears and uncertainties.

'Good.' She was trying hard to let nothing show in her eyes but he was staring at her impatiently.

'Is it? Because it doesn't sound like it to me.'

He moved swiftly round the table, stopping in front of her. The paleness of her face made her eyes seem incredibly green, and he ran his hand over his face, needing action to counteract the ache in his chest, unsure of his footing in this uncharted territory.

'Teddie…' He softened his voice.

She lifted one hand to her throat and raised the other in front of her, as though warding him off. It was a gesture of such conflicting vulnerability and defiance that he was suddenly struggling to breathe.

'I'm not just saying what I think you want to hear.'

'I know.' She gave him a small, sad smile. 'And I want you to be there for George. It's just it's only ever been me and him. I know you're his father, but I've never had to share him before and it feels like a big deal.'

Aristo stared down at her. The fact that Teddie

loved her son so fiercely made something wrench apart inside his chest and, taking a step forward, he pulled her gently towards him.

'I'm not going to take him away from you, Teddie,' he said softly. 'I couldn't even if I wanted to. You're his mother. But I want to be the best father I can be. The best *man* I can be.'

He felt some of the tension ease out of her spine and shoulders, and then, leaning forward unsteadily, she rested her head against his chest.

Listening to the solid beat of his heart, Teddie felt her body start to soften, adrenalin dissolving in her blood, his clean masculine scent filling her chest.

The air around them was suddenly heavy and charged. She felt weightless, lost in the moment and in him, so that without thinking she curled her arms around his body, her fingers following the contours of the muscles of his back. And then she was pushing up his T-shirt and touching smooth, warm skin.

His hand was sliding rhythmically through her hair, tipping her head back, and his mouth was brushing over her cheeks and lips like the softest feathers, teasing her so that she could hear her own breathing inside her head, like the waves rushing inside a seashell.

She took a breath, her hands splaying out, wanting more of his skin, his heat, his smooth, hard muscle. Her heart was pounding, the longing inside of her combusting as she felt the fingers of his other hand travel lightly over her bare back. And then her stomach clenched as he parted her lips and kissed her open-mouthed, his tongue so warm and soft and teasing that she felt the lick of heat slide through her like a flame.

Her head was swimming.

She wanted more—more of his mouth, his touch, his skin—so much more of him. Reaching up, she clasped his face, kissing him back, pulling him closer, lifting her hips and oscillating against him, trying, needing to relieve the ache radiating from her pelvis.

Heat was spilling over her skin and, arching upwards, she felt his breath stumble, and then he was sliding a hand through her hair, holding her captive as he kissed her more deeply, his warm breath filling her mouth so that she was melting from the inside out.

Her fingers were scrabbling against his skin… She moaned…

There was a second of agonising pulsing stillness, and then slowly she felt him pull away.

His eyes were dark with passion. For a moment he didn't speak, and she knew as he breathed out roughly that he was looking for the right words, looking for *any* words because he was as stunned as she.

'Sorry. I didn't mean to do that.'

She stared up at him, an ache like thirst spreading outwards. 'Me neither.'

'So I suppose we should just forget it ever happened.'

He made it sound like a statement, but she knew it was a question from the dark and unblinking intensity of his gaze. Suddenly she could barely breathe.

Should they? Would it really be so very bad to press her foot down on the accelerator pedal and run the red light just once?

She could feel something inside her shifting and softening, and the urge to reach out was so intense and pure that she almost cried out. But her need for him couldn't be trusted on so many levels— not least the fact that no man had come close to filling the emptiness that she'd been ignoring for four years.

'I think that would be for the best,' she said quickly, lifting her gaze, her green eyes meeting his. 'Just be a father to him.'

His steady, knowing gaze made her heartbeat falter and she glanced away, up to a near perfect moon, glowing pearlescent in the darkening sky.

'Thank you for a lovely evening, but I should probably go and check on George.'

And, taking a fast, hard breath, she sidestepped past him and walked on shaking legs towards the villa.

In the darkness of her son's room she leaned against the wall, seeking solace in its cool surface.

She shouldn't have agreed with him.

She should have told him that he was wrong.

Then remembering his open laptop, she tensed. They might have called a ceasefire, but she still didn't trust him.

And it wasn't just Aristo she didn't trust. She didn't trust herself either.

Four years ago she'd let her libido overrule not just her common sense but every instinct she'd had, and it had been a disaster. Nothing had changed except this time she knew the score.

Aristo might be the only man who had made her body sing, but she knew now that if she allowed herself to be intimate with him then she ran the risk of getting hurt—and she'd worked so hard to un-love him.

So that left friendship. Not the sort of easy affection and solidarity that she shared with Elliot, but the polite formality of former lovers now sidestepping around each other's lives and new partners.

Her heart lurched as visions of Aristo with a new wife flooded her head and she felt suddenly sick. It had been hard enough getting over him last time. Far worse though was the thought of having to witness him sharing his life with someone else.

CHAPTER SIX

IT WAS THE most perfect peach Teddie had ever seen. Perfectly plump, sunset-coloured, it was half concealed by a cluster of pale green leaves, like a shy swimmer hiding behind a towel on the beach.

She'd spotted it yesterday evening, when she and George had joined the housekeeper, Melina, as she'd wandered around the garden, choosing ingredients for the evening meal. In the end they had collected fat, dark-skinned figs to go with the salty feta and thyme-scented honey that had followed a dessert of delicious homemade strawberry ice-cream—George's favourite.

She let out a quiver of breath, remembering her son's reaction as she'd told him that Aristo was his father. Watching his face shift from confusion to shy understanding, she'd felt her heart twist—as it was twisting now at the memory, although not with regret. And she knew George had no regrets either, for he was happily 'helping' Melina crack eggs for the *strapatsada* they were having for breakfast.

Standing on tiptoe, she stretched out her arm, her fingers almost touching the peach's skin. If only she was just a little bit taller...

She breathed in sharply as a hand stole past her and gently pulled the peach free.

'Hey!' Turning, she stared up at Aristo in outrage. 'That's mine.'

He looked her straight in the eye and kept on looking. 'Not according to the evidence.'

Her fingers twitched. She was tempted to make a grab for it, but already his proximity was sending her senses haywire and she didn't want to risk reaching out to touch the *wrong* soft, golden flesh...

She swallowed. Her desire for him chewed at her constantly, and already her insides felt so soft and warm it was as if she was melting.

Watching the play of emotions cross her face, Aristo felt his body tense. He could sense the conflict in her and it was driving him crazy. For once they'd had only to be alone and they would be reaching for one another—his hand circling her waist, her fingers sliding over his shoulders...

His blood seemed to slow and thicken and his limbs felt suddenly light as he stared at her profile, at the dark arch of her eyebrow above the straight line of her nose and the full curving mouth. There was a sprinkle of freckles across her cheeks and he wanted to reach out and touch each and every one.

Instead, though, he glanced down at the peach, turning it over in his hand, his thumb tracing the cleft in the downy flesh. 'What will you give me for it?' he asked softly, his mouth curving upwards.

Teddie swallowed. This was Aristo at his most dangerous. That combination of tantalising smile and teasing dark, dark eyes. And, even though she knew she shouldn't, she held his gaze and said lightly, 'How about I *don't* push you into that lavender bush if you hand it over?'

Laughing, he held out the peach. 'And I was going to offer to share it with you.'

His fingers brushed against hers as she took the peach and she felt a tremor down her spine like a charge of electricity. 'So let's share it,' she said casually. 'There's a knife in that basket.'

'Are you sure it won't spoil your appetite?'

A suspended silence seemed to saturate the air around them and, staring past him, she said quickly, 'The basket's on the bench.'

She watched as carefully he halved the peach, then pitted and sliced it, his profile a pure gold line against the intense blue sky. The creamy golden flesh was still warm from the sun and heavy with juice, and as she bit into it the intense sweetness ricocheted around her mouth.

'Wow! They don't taste like that in New York.'

Folding the knife, he dropped it back into the basket. 'No, they don't. But then everything tastes better here.'

She frowned at the edge that had entered his voice. 'You make that sound like a *bad* thing.'

A light breeze stirred between them and the air

felt suddenly over-warm, the sunlight suddenly over-bright.

He shrugged. 'It's not a bad thing—just a consequence of living in a fantasy. When you go back to civilisation, reality doesn't quite match up.'

Her heart was pounding against her chest. He was referring to the peach, but he might easily have been talking about their marriage—for wasn't that what had happened? They had married on impulse, without really knowing anything about one another—certainly not enough to make till-death-do-us-part vows. And even before the honeymoon had been over it had become clear to both of them that what they'd shared in all those hotel rooms across America was too fragile to survive real life.

And yet here they both were in this idyllic sun-drenched garden sharing a peach.

She felt a flutter of hope. Okay, this wasn't real life, but they weren't newly weds either and Aristo wanted to make this work. They both did. And that was the difference between now and then. Four years ago they hadn't wanted the same things, but that had been before George.

Remembering how at breakfast Aristo had answered their son's questions about his motorboat patiently, giving him his full attention, she released a pent-up breath.

'I think you're looking at it the wrong way,' she

said slowly. 'I mean, peaches in New York might not taste like the peaches here—but what about the cheesecake? You can't tell me that they have cheesecake here like they do at Eileen's.'

He frowned. 'I wouldn't know. I've never eaten there. Actually, I've never had cheesecake.'

'Really?' Teddie stared at him in disbelief. 'Well, that's not right. As soon as we get back to New York we're going out to have to fix that.'

Aristo laughed. 'We are?'

He seemed pleased.

'They do all kinds of flavours. When I was pregnant I had these terrible cravings for baked cheesecake and it just kind of carried on. Now it's a regular thing. Last Saturday in the month. You could come too.'

'It's a date,' he said softly.

Her heart was suddenly beating too fast. 'I didn't mean just the two of us,' she said quickly.

Was that how it had sounded? Or was he just accepting her invitation?

Aristo held her gaze, but the anticipation that had been flickering through his veins had abruptly dissolved. His shoulders tensed. After the moment of intimacy the swift rejection was unsettling, but it was the confirmation he needed that he couldn't be casual with her in the way he'd been with other women in his life.

She had been his wife, and he was determined

that she would be again. Only, he wasn't going to get emotionally played.

He turned and looked at her, his expression unreadable. 'Of course not. Are you supposed to be picking something for Melina?'

Reaching down, he picked up the basket and she nodded, grateful for a shift in conversation.

'Yes, I was—lemons and thyme.'

For a moment she thought he was going to offer to help her. Instead, though, he held the basket out to her. 'Then I'll leave you to it.'

And before she had a chance to respond he had turned and was walking back towards the villa.

'Hurry up, Mommy.'

For the second time in so many minutes Teddie felt George's hand tug at the edge of her shorts.

'I'm trying, sweetie. Just let me check this one last pocket.'

Fumbling in the side of her suitcase, she smiled distractedly down at her son, who was sitting on the floor of her dressing room.

Her hat was great when she was sitting on the sun lounger, but it was difficult to wear in the pool and she was trying to find the hairbands that she'd packed—or at least thought she'd packed—so that she could put her hair up to protect her head.

'Mommy, come *on*!'

'Darling, the pool will still be there—' she said soothingly,

But, shaking his head, George interrupted her. 'I don't want to go to the pool. I want to see the pirate boat.'

Pirate boat! What pirate boat?

Giving up on her search, she pushed the case back into the wardrobe and turned to where George was sitting on the floor beside a selection of toy vehicles, his upturned eyes watching her anxiously.

'What are you talking about, darling?' Gently, she pushed a curl away from his forehead.

'The pirate boat.' He bit his lip, clearly baffled by his mother's confusion. 'Aristo—I mean, *Daddy...*'

He paused, and her heart turned over as he looked up at her. The word was not yet automatic to him.

'They left it behind and Daddy said he'd take us to see it.'

Teddie frowned. She had some vague memory of Aristo talking about pirates when they were eating breakfast that morning, but she'd been only half paying attention, she thought guiltily. Most of her head had still been spinning from that almost-kiss they'd shared last night.

'Okay—well, we can do that. I was just going to tie my hair back.' Leaning forward, she gave him an impish grin. 'But I've had a much better idea!'

Ten minutes later she was walking through the villa with George scampering by her side. Both of them were wearing blue and white striped T-shirts and Teddie had drawn a moustache and stubble on their faces.

'Shall we scare him?' George whispered, accelerating into a little run.

He seemed giddy with excitement at the prospect, and Teddie nodded. But as they crept out onto the terrace the giggle she'd been holding back subsided as she saw that the pool was empty.

'Where is he?' George's hand tightened around hers and instinctively she gave it a squeeze.

'He's probably getting changed.' She gave him a reassuring smile.

Ten minutes later, though, they were still waiting by the pool.

'Do you think he's forgotten?' George whispered.

He was starting to look anxious, and she couldn't stop a flicker of uncertainty rippling down her spine.

She shook her head. 'No, of course not,' she said firmly. 'Why don't we give it another five minutes and then we'll go and look for him? I'm sure he'll be here any moment.'

But Aristo didn't arrive. Finally, Teddie took George's hand, and they walked back into the villa just as Melina came rushing towards them.

'I was coming to find you! I completely forgot Mr Aristo said that he was going to be in his office. He has a very important work call.'

Nodding, Teddie pinned a smile on her face, but inside she could feel a rising swell of angry disappointment as she asked Melina to take George to the kitchen. Disappointment and relief—for hadn't she been expecting this to happen?

She bit down on her misery. An important work call! No, scratch that, a *very* important work call, she thought bitterly. Her throat tightened. Had she really thought that things could be different? Or that Aristo could change? She should have realised how this holiday was going to pan out that first morning, when she'd spotted his laptop crouching like some alien in the blazing Mediterranean sunshine. But, idiot that she was, she'd assumed it was a one-off.

Aristo's office wasn't hard to find, and his voice was clearly audible as she walked stiffly up to the open door.

'No, we need total transparency. I *want* total transparency—exactly.'

He was standing by his desk, his phone tucked against his ear, the tension in his body at odds with the casual informality of his clothing. She stepped into the room, her heartbeat ringing in her ears as he looked up from his laptop, his frown of concentration fading.

'I'm going to have to call you back, Nick,' he said quietly. Hanging up, he stared at Teddie impassively. 'So you got my message?'

'Loud and clear,' she snapped. Stalking into the room, she stopped in front of the desk. 'I was a bit stunned at first, but I suppose it wasn't that much of a surprise. You put work first during the whole of our marriage, so why should a holiday to get to know your son be any different?'

His face creased into a frown. 'I don't know what you're talking about. It's *one* call—'

Her response to his words was instant, visceral, making her heartbeat accelerate, emotion clog her throat. It was everything she'd dreaded—only it had happened so much more quickly than even she had thought possible. Literally within hours of him claiming that he wanted to be there for her and George.

But how many times had her father made just such a claim?

'I'm talking about *this*,' she interrupted him. 'About you, sneaking off to close some deal—'

She broke off abruptly. The misery inside her chest was like a block of ice and she was starting to feel sick.

Aristo felt the pulse of anger start to beat beneath his skin. Ever since they'd told George that he was his father Teddie had been acting strangely, oscillating between a suspended tangible hunger and a maddening aloofness, but this—her anger, her baseless accusation—was so unexpected, so unfair.

And she was dressed as a pirate—although clearly she had forgotten that fact.

Just at that moment his phone started to ring and, glancing up at the ceiling, she rolled her eyes in a way that made him want to find a plank and make her walk it.

'I'm not going to answer that,' he said coolly. 'And I wasn't *sneaking* anywhere. Something important came up and I needed to deal with it. I told Melina to give you a message, and she did.'

Why was this so hard for her to understand? He'd taken a week off work, but that didn't mean his business was on hold. And who did she think he was doing all this for—and why? Women might talk about needing love and being loved, but what that translated into was a relentless desire for money and status—as his mother had proved.

His phone was still ringing and her green eyes narrowed like a cat's. 'We're not some junior members of your staff you can just fob off.'

'I wasn't fobbing you off.'

She stared at him incredulously. 'George is *three years old*, Aristo. He was so excited.' Her voice quivered and she paused, then straightened her shoulders determinedly. 'You didn't even give him a second thought, did you? But the thing about three-year-olds is that if you say you're going to do something then you have to do it. You can't lie to him.'

His phone had finally stopped ringing, but his chest felt suddenly so tight that he couldn't breathe.

'That's rich—coming from you.'

He watched the colour drain from her face, but he told himself that she deserved it.

'You lied to him from the day he was born. And you lied to me too.' He shook his head dismissively. 'All those years, and not once did you consider telling me the truth.'

'That's not true.' Her face blazing with anger, Teddie took a step forward. 'I did try and tell you.'

'Don't give me that.' The coldness in his eyes made her stomach churn. 'You could have contacted me in any number of ways.'

'I did,' she said flatly, the flame of her anger dying as quickly as it had ignited, smothered by the memory of the phone calls she'd made to his various offices around the globe, and the polite but cool indifference of the Leonidas staff.

'I tried them all. By the time I realised I was pregnant, you'd left America, so I tried calling you, but you blocked me on your phone, so then I called your offices and left messages with your staff asking you to call me back but you never did. And I wrote to you, every year on George's birthday but I never got a reply.'

There was a long silence.

Aristo could feel his heart pounding, the shock of her words pricking his skin like bee stings. She was telling the truth. He could hear it in the matter-of-fact tone of her voice. And yes, he *had* blocked her number, told his staff not to bother him with any kind of communications from Teddie... And they had done what they'd been told. But he'd been angry and hurt—and also scared that if he even so much as heard her voice he would do something stupid, like listen to his heart...

He'd just wanted to put it all behind him—to forget her and his marriage—

'So you gave up?' His pride might have contributed to him not finding out about his son, but the bulk of the responsibility was still hers.

Watching her eyes widen with anger and astonishment, seeing the sudden shine of tears, he felt harsh, cruel—only before he could say anything she took a step towards him.

'Yes, I gave up! Because I was on my own and I was sick and I was scared.' She breathed out unsteadily. 'But even if I hadn't given up, and you had got my messages, you wouldn't have called me anyway. No doubt something *very important* at work would have come up and you'd have had to deal with that instead.'

He stared at her in silence, his face set and tense, his dark eyes narrowing like arrowheads. 'Not this again.' He shook his head. 'Unlike you, Teddie, I'm not a magician. I can't just pull a hotel out of a hat and take a bow. I work on global projects that employ tens of thousands of people. I have responsibilities, commitments.'

His face looked cold and businesslike. It was the face he'd used on her when he'd been late home from work, or cancelled dinner, or spent all weekend on the phone. Behind him, through the window, the flat, shifting blues of the Mediterranean seemed an oddly serene backdrop to their heated argument.

'*Responsibilities...commitments...*' Her voice echoed his words incredulously. 'Yes, you do, Aristo. Four years ago you had a wife—me—and now you have a son—George.'

'I was working to build up the business for you, so you didn't have to worry about money!'

Surely she could understand his motives for working so hard? Had they stayed together she would have been the first to complain, for women were never satisfied with just enough—they always wanted more.

'Well, I didn't marry you for your money.'

He heard the catch in her voice and his chest tightened as he watched her lip tremble.

'And you're already fantastically wealthy. So why are you still working as though your life depends on it?'

There was a short, strained silence, and then, as his phone started to ring again, she took a deep breath.

'You should probably answer that,' she said quietly. 'We clearly have nothing left to say.'

And, turning, she walked swiftly out of the room.

Twenty minutes later, having got directions from Melina, she and George reached the right cove. The pirate boat was at the back of the beach on the dunes, its wooden hull bleached like the bones of some marine animal. It was more of a rowing boat than an actual pirate ship with masts, but it was still recognisably a boat and, on seeing it, George began towing her down the dunes.

'Look, Mommy, *look*!'

'I can see it, darling,' she said quickly.

He'd been unusually quiet during the walk, and she was grateful to hear a hint of his former excitement back in his voice.

After walking out of Aristo's office she had collected him from the kitchen, explaining in an over-bright voice that, 'Daddy is very sorry that he can't come right now, but he wants us to go without him.'

Watching her son's face fall, she had wanted to storm back into Aristo's office, snatch his phone and hurl it out of the window along with his laptop. She knew exactly how George was feeling, and the fact that *she* had somehow let it happen, by letting her selfish, workaholic ex-husband into his life, felt like a dagger between her ribs.

'Do you want to have a look inside?' she whispered.

He nodded and, leaning down, she picked him up. They inspected the ship carefully, but aside from a few small startled crabs they found nothing.

George sighed and, glancing down at him, she saw that his eyes were shining with tears. With an intensity that hurt, she wished she had planned ahead and hidden something for him to find.

'Daddy would know where the treasure is,' he said sadly.

She breathed out silently. *But Daddy isn't here. He's holed up his office, expanding his empire.*

'He might—but we haven't really looked properly. And most treasure is buried, isn't it?' she said reasonably.

'Yes, it is,' said a familiar male voice as a shadow fell across her. 'And no self-respecting pirate would ever leave his treasure lying about on his ship.'

'Daddy!'

George launched himself at his father.

Looking up at Aristo, Teddie felt her heartbeat accelerate. He was wearing a white shirt unbuttoned at the neck, and a pair of rolled-up dark trousers. He'd borrowed what looked like a scarf and tied it bandana-style around his head. The stubble, however, was his own.

He looked incredibly sexy—but she wasn't about to let his looks or her libido wipe the slate clean, and nor was she about to expose George to any further disappointment.

'I think we should be getting back now,' she said stiffly. 'We can look for treasure another time.'

Their eyes met, and she glared at him above George's head.

'Trust me,' he said softly. 'I've got this.'

He headed off along the beach with George scampering beside him. Gritting her teeth, she watched them crouch down near a rocky outcrop, then stand up again. And now they were heading back towards her.

'Mommy, *look*!'

George was jumping up and down, and even at a distance she could see that his eyes were wide with excitement.

'I'm coming,' she called.

She half-walked, half-ran across the sand, to where he was pointing excitedly at a large white stone clearly marked with an *X*. Her heart seemed to slide sideways and she glanced up at Aristo in confusion.

The sun was behind his head, casting a shadow across his face, but she could feel his eyes, sense their intensity, and suddenly she understood what he'd done.

'We must have walked right past it,' she said, when she was completely sure her voice was composed.

Aristo lifted the stone, and then he and George scooped out sand with their hands until finally their fingers found the edges of a wooden box. To Teddie's eyes it was obviously far too well-preserved to be a pirate's relic, but she could see that her son had no doubt that it was genuine.

She watched him pull it free, and open it.

'Oh, George,' she whispered. The box was filled with gleaming golden coins. 'You are so lucky.'

He looked up at her, his face trembling with astonishment. 'Can I take it home?'

'Of course.' Reaching out, Aristo cupped his son's chin in his hand. 'This is my island, and you're my son, and everything I have is yours.'

Back at the villa, they ate early. George was exhausted, and could barely keep his eyes open, so Aristo put him to bed and then joined Teddie on the terrace.

There was a short, delicate pause.

'I wanted to say thank you for earlier,' she said quietly. 'It was magical, and so thoughtful of you.'

'All I can say is that real pirates had it easy.' He groaned. 'Honestly, cleaning those coins nearly killed me. It took so *long*.'

She laughed. 'Aristo Leonidas wearing his fingers to the bone! I really wish I'd seen that.'

His eyes on hers were suddenly serious. 'Well, I'm glad you didn't. It was my turn to make magic happen for you.' His mouth twisted. 'I'm sorry about the phone call.'

'I'm sorry too.' She squeezed his hand. 'I shouldn't have jumped to conclusions.'

'You didn't. I took the call and I shouldn't have done,' he said simply.

Turning his gaze towards the blue sheet of water below, Aristo frowned. Crossing the dunes earlier, his breath had seemed to choke him, and with every step he'd grown more convinced that he'd blown it.

Now, though, beneath a pink sunset, with Teddie sitting opposite him wearing that same simple sundress, his reaction seemed ludicrously out of proportion.

Or it would have done but for the unasked question that was reverberating inside his head and had been since she'd stormed out of his office.

'Did you mean it?' he said abruptly. 'Did you mean what you said earlier—about not marrying me for my money?'

He could see the confusion in her eyes. 'Yes, of course. I would have married you if you'd been penniless.'

'So why did you keep working, then?' Another question—this one older, but just as pressing. 'In New York?'

She frowned. 'I needed to—I need to have that control.'

The words left her mouth unprompted, unedited, and she stared at him, embarrassed and angry, because up until that moment that fact had been private, not something she could even really admit to herself.

Sensing his curiosity, she hesitated, but his dark gaze was calm and unfazed and she felt her heartbeat steady itself.

'My mum was terrible with money. She was so out of it sometimes she'd forget to pay the rent. And she was always upping her medication, so it would run out, and then we'd have to buy other people's prescriptions. Otherwise she'd steal them.' She swallowed. 'I know my life isn't like that any more, but...'

Gazing down, she saw that her hands were clenched in her lap, and with an effort she forced her fingers apart.

'I can't seem to stop that feeling of dread.'

'I didn't know that was how you felt,' he said slowly.

She shrugged. 'Having a regular income, however small, just makes me feel calmer.' Finishing her sentence, she glanced towards the door. 'We should probably go back in.'

For a moment Aristo didn't respond, and then he nodded slowly and they stood up and walked back through the silent house.

'You asked me why I work. And you're right—it's not the money, or even how work makes me feel…'

He had stopped at the top of the stairs and was staring back down, as though considering his next step, his next sentence. Finally he turned to face her.

'I do like being in control…having a focus—but it's more than that. It's about creating something that matters beyond just making me rich.' His gaze fixed on her face. 'I want my brand, my name—George's name now—to be indelible.'

And he was prepared to work relentlessly to reach his goal, Teddie thought miserably. Even when he was just talking about it, she could see the fire in his eyes, the relentlessness and determination to succeed, and her stomach clenched. How could she or George compete with that?

As though reading her thoughts, he shook his head. 'I know what you're thinking. And you're right. Work was too important to me—more than it should have been. But only because I let it be. I can change. I'm already changing.'

He took a step forward and his fingers brushed against hers lightly, then he caught her hand in his.

'We both are. Look at us talking.'

His hand tightened around hers and he sounded so vehement that she found herself smiling.

It was true. Last time he had stonewalled her,

and she had run away rather than face their problems, but here they were discussing things. Only…

'Aristo, I'm glad we're talking, but…' She hesitated. 'I'm not sure that's enough for us to find a way back to how we used to be.'

'Good.' He pulled her against him so that suddenly their eyes were level. 'Because I don't want what we had before. What we had before needed improving. This time you and George are going to be my top priority.'

Her heart was beating too fast; she couldn't keep up with him. Or with the rush of longing that was racing through her blood. 'Did *everything* about us need improving?'

His dark gaze rested on her face. 'No, I can think of one thing at least that was utterly incomparable,' he said softly. 'But if you don't believe me then maybe I could remind you.'

His words rippled over her skin like the softest caress. He looked so handsome, so certain. She could feel the smooth tension of his hard body next to hers, and his eyes were darker than the night sky. She knew she should disentangle herself, but instead she reached up and touched his face.

She heard him breathe out softly, and the sound made something inside her chest crack apart like ice breaking. She wanted him so badly that she felt she might catch fire. So why was she fighting it? Fighting herself? What point was she really proving to Aristo, or herself, by denying the attraction between them?

They already had a bond through George. Nothing could be more permanent and binding than a child, and she had managed to come to terms with that by setting boundaries.

So stop making everything way more complicated than it needs to be, she told herself. *Than you want it to be.*

His hand was firm against her waist, his eyes steady on her face, and she could feel his longing, sense the power beneath his skin. But she knew that he was holding himself back, waiting for permission.

She ran her finger along the line of his jaw and tilted his head down so that their mouths were almost touching. 'I don't need reminding,' she whispered.

His mouth brushed against hers, barely touching, teasing her, and his hand slid up to cup her breast, his fingertips grazing her nipple. Feeling the swell of blood beneath her skin, she breathed in sharply, leaning into him, and then, taking his other hand, she led him slowly towards his bedroom.

They were just over the threshold when he pulled back, then stopped, his eyes narrowed, his face taut with concentration.

'Is this what you want, Teddie?' he said hoarsely. 'Me…this?'

She stared at him in silence, her body throbbing.

Maybe it was just the island working its magic on her, subtly, irresistibly, but it—*he*—was what she wanted.

'Yes.'

In one swift movement he pushed the door shut and, leaning forward, kissed her fiercely, his hand sliding up beneath her hair to cup her head, his kisses spilling like warm liquid over her mouth and throat and breast.

The touch of his warm mouth was making everything tingle and tighten, so that she could hardly bear it. She moaned softly and then her body started to shake and she began pulling at his clothes, her hands clumsy with desire.

Sucking in a breath, he lifted his mouth and, stepping back, peeled off his shirt, reached for his shorts.

'No, wait, let me,' she said hoarsely.

His eyes narrowed in protest, but as she reached out and ran her fingertips over the muscles of his stomach he stayed still. Gently, she caressed his smooth skin, following the path of dark hair down to his waistband, then lower still. As she traced the thickness of his erection, feeling it twitch and swell and harden beneath his shorts, she heard him groan and felt his hand lock in her hair.

Slowly, carefully, she undid the cord around his waist and pulled him free. Heart thudding, she stared at him in silence, her mouth dry, her breath quickening.

'My turn now,' he said softly.

His fingers were light but firm. Unbuttoning her dress, he let it slip to the floor and breathed in sharply. She was wearing no bra, just a pair of the palest peach panties, and her body was flecked with sand. He stared at her, spellbound, and then, taking her hand, he led her into the bathroom and pulled her into the shower.

As his hands spread over her ribs, Teddie closed her eyes. Warm water was trickling over her skin and her belly was tight and hot and aching. She curled her hands into his wet hair, reaching out for his hard, muscular body, trying to shake some of the dizziness in her head. She wanted him so much, wanted the ache inside her to be satisfied, and helplessly she arched up against him, pressing, pulling, pleading with her fingers…

But as he lowered his mouth and sucked fiercely on her nipples she gasped, stepping unsteadily back against the wall of the shower.

Aristo stilled, the soft sound bringing him to his senses. Closing his mind against the heavy, insistent beat of hunger in his groin, he lifted his head. 'Are you protected?'

She stared at him dazedly, then shook her head.

Groaning, he backed out of the shower, his heart pounding. When he returned she had stripped off her panties and his body stiffened in instant response. Gritting his teeth, he rolled the condom on and then kissed her again, parting her lips, plundering her mouth with his tongue. His hands were roaming over her belly and between her thighs and, feeling her move against his fingers, he was suddenly struggling to breathe.

Teddie moaned softly. Her body was aching now and, reaching out, her hand found his erection. Hardly breathing, she slid her fingers over the rigid, pulsing length, pulling him closer, opening her legs. She heard him breathe in raggedly and then he was lifting her up, bracing himself against the wall. Shifting against him, panting, she guided him inch by inch into her trembling body to where a ball of heat was starting to implode.

Flattening himself against her, Aristo began to thrust, out of sync at first, then in time to the pulse beating in his head. His mouth found hers and he felt her respond, deepening the kiss. His heartbeat was accelerating and, closing his eyes, he felt his body start to cut loose from its moorings. Teddie arched upwards, her hands gripping his shoulders, nails cutting into the muscle. He felt her tense, heard her cry out, and then his body shuddered and he erupted into her.

CHAPTER SEVEN

IT WAS EARLY when Teddie woke up. She wasn't sure what time it was, but as she opened her eyes she could tell from the pale wash of light spreading through the room that dawn was not far away.

She blinked. They must have forgotten to close the shutters—but then they'd had no thought for anything except each other. Her face grew hot as she remembered how Aristo had stripped her naked, his hands smooth against her skin, smooth and hard and urgent.

How she had needed his touch, craved the frenzy of release that he alone had given her. And she had wanted to touch him too, splaying her fingers over his body, pressing her thumbs into the muscles of his shoulders and down his back, her hands shaking with eagerness.

Glancing over at Aristo, she felt her breath still in her throat. He was deeply asleep, his long dark lashes grazing his cheekbones, one arm loosely curling over the pillow. She loved how smooth his skin was—and his smell: salt and sunlight and some kind of citrus. She lay for a moment, trying to hear his heartbeat in the silence, feeling the gravitational pull of his body.

And she would have carried on lying there, except that her mouth felt dry, and there was a sharp ache beneath her ribs, like thirst only more intense. Pushing back the sheet carefully, so as not to wake him, she slid out of bed.

Tiptoeing into the bathroom, she turned on the tap and, grabbing her hair to one side, held her mouth open beneath the running water. It tasted good and she swallowed greedily, and then, standing up, she caught a glimpse of her reflection in the mirror.

She stilled. She had been fighting herself for days now, and giving in to her desire had felt like such a big step, with such serious, far-reaching consequences, that she had expected to see a sign. But then when it had finally happened she had never felt more certain of anything—except when she'd found out she was pregnant and had decided to keep the baby.

Some things were just meant to be, and leading him into his bedroom had given her a peace that came from being part of something greater and beyond her control.

And now? How did she feel *now*?

She searched anxiously inside herself for feelings of regret—but how could she regret what had happened last night? He'd felt so right against her, their bodies seamless against one another, and even now the memory of his touch made her head swim. It had been wonderful, incredible... The corners of her mouth turned up and she realised she was grinning stupidly at herself in the mirror. *Magical!*

And it wasn't just the sex. She'd been there before, tumbling into bed with Aristo after that meeting with their lawyers, but then it had felt so different—off-key, every word a misstep, their bodies desperately seeking a way to resolve what they hadn't even tried to address.

Only, now they'd talked—really talked—and there had been no desperation, just a sense of irrefutable rightness.

So, no, she didn't regret any of it—but nor, she realised, had the ache in her chest subsided. It wasn't water she wanted.

Back in the bedroom, she slipped under the sheets and felt him shift beside her. Gazing down, she saw that his eyes were open, and then his hand was sliding over her stomach and her body rippled into life and she reached for him urgently.

An ivory-coloured light greeted Aristo when he blinked his eyes open several hours later. For a few moments he lay on his back, watching the white muslin curtain flutter weakly in the barely there breeze, and then slowly he stretched out his arms above his head.

For days now, ever since he'd walked into the Kildare lounge and spotted Teddie, his body had been on edge, vibrating with the muscle memory of what it had been like to hold his ex-wife in his arms, to feel her body arching beneath his and hear her soft gasp of climax.

Last night had transformed memory into reality, and now, lying among the warm mussed-up bedding, breathing in the scent of her skin, his body was already craving her again.

Unsurprisingly.

Right from the moment she'd reached for him he'd been enslaved. And not just by her beauty or the way her body had melted into his. She'd taken the heaviness from his heart, made the blood run more lightly in his veins, and he'd never met anyone like her before or since.

Despite the undeniable attraction between them, Teddie had been keeping him at arm's length. Until last night, when she had led him to his bedroom and he had felt like an exile returning to the promised land.

He breathed out once, then got up swiftly and walked into the bathroom. Stepping under the shower, he closed his eyes, tipping his head back under the warm water, and instantly he felt his body harden, his brain dazzled by the memory of Teddie naked, sliding down his body, cupping him in her mouth—

His eyes snapped open and he punched off the water. It still didn't feel real: to be able to touch her again, to have her consent to kiss and caress her freely, to stretch out her body beneath his.

But it had happened.

And the relief was unimaginable—as intoxicating and potent as wine. And even more potent was the knowledge that she had felt the same way too. Even if she hadn't stated her desire out loud, he'd have felt the urgency in her, felt a need as explicit and unequivocal as his own, and the tautness of her nipples and the slick heat between her thighs had been answer enough.

And holding her whilst she slept… He had liked it that she had curled against him, had enjoyed almost against his will the possessive feeling it had provoked, even though it was the kind of primitive he-man response he would normally despise.

But it was daunting, knowing how easy it would be to lose himself in Teddie. Look at how he was feeling now. Already he could feel the previously insurmountable barriers around his heart starting to crack apart, like pack ice feeling a spring sun.

Only, that wasn't going to happen.

Not this time.

Yes, he wanted Teddie back in his bed fulltime. But now, knowing now what he did about her childhood, he knew what was required to make her stay there—she needed stability and certainty, something vast and unshakable, and with his business about to go public he was in a position to give her and George what they deserved.

Because last night hadn't been just about sex.

A muscle flickered in his jaw. It had been about momentum and, just like in business, once you had momentum that was the time to push on to the next step.

In Teddie's case that meant convincing her to marry him.

Outside, he heard George's voice and Teddie's reply. Instantly his skin was prickling, his heart bumping against his ribs as he walked out of his bedroom, down the stairs and into the brilliant sunshine.

Teddie was leaning forward, laying the table, her dark hair swinging loosely across her shoulders, and in her pale pink sleeveless blouse and sawn-off denim shorts she looked like a very sexy castaway. Beside her, George was eating a bowl of yoghurt.

'Daddy—Daddy, we're having…we're having…' Looking up from his breakfast, George hesitated, a small frown of concentration creasing his forehead. 'What are we having, Mommy?'

Glancing over to where Aristo was standing behind her son, Teddie felt her heart start to beat unevenly.

Waking for the second time, she had found it agonisingly hard to leave the lambent warmth of Aristo's body. But she'd had no choice. Like most young children, George woke early and, although he'd been sleeping in longer since they'd arrived on the island, she hadn't wanted to risk him waking up and discovering her bed empty.

Her pulse fluttered forward like a startled deer.

Or, worse, waking up and finding her in Aristo's room.

Daylight hadn't changed her mind. But although she was willing—eager, in fact—to share his bed, she had no illusions. Sublime sex hadn't been enough to save their marriage four years ago, and it was not enough to rebuild their relationship now.

That didn't mean that she regretted what had happened. On the contrary, she knew it would happen again and she wanted it to—because she wanted him: the one, the only man whose touch left her begging for release.

Especially here, on this beautiful island paradise. Here they were far away from the demands of real life, and it was easy to live in the moment and not think further. And when it ended, as it undoubtedly would, when they returned to New York, she would move on with her life.

So why expose George to this sudden temporary change to her sleeping arrangements? He was three years old. Plus, he'd only just found out that Aristo was his father and, although he'd taken it very well, she understood enough about children—

and her son in particular—to know that it was a huge, *permanent* tectonic change to his life.

Besides, he had no understanding of sex, let alone the complex dynamics of his parents' relationship, so how could she hope to explain that she and his father hadn't loved each other enough to make their marriage work, but the sexual charge between them was too powerful to resist?

The thought of trying to do so made her brain feel as though it was being pressed in a vice.

She cleared her throat. '*Pites*—I think that's what Melina said they're called.' She forced herself to look at Aristo.

He nodded. 'You mean the little pies?' Reaching down, he ruffled George's hair. 'They used to be my favourite when I was your age. They're delicious.'

George twisted round to look at Teddie. 'I want to have them *now*, Mommy.'

He tugged at her hand and she let him pull her from her chair. 'Well, I don't know if they're ready...'

'Can I go and ask Melina? Can I?'

Her arm tightened around her son but, resisting the urge to draw him against her leg like a shield, she nodded. 'Don't run—and don't forget to say please,' she called after him.

There was a small sea breeze shimmying across the terrace and she tucked a stray strand of hair behind her ear. She knew she should say something, only she couldn't think of a single word.

As Aristo took a step closer she felt a rush of panic. What if he tried to kiss her and George saw?

Edging behind the table, she gave him what she hoped was a casual smile. 'Did your mother make them?'

'Make what?'

He stared at her in a way that made her muscles tense. Not quite hostile, but wary. Her smile stiffened, her heartbeat suddenly swift-moving, erratic.

'The pies?' she prompted. 'You said they were your favourite when you were George's age. I thought your mother…' Her voice faded. His expression hadn't altered outwardly, but there was a slight tension in his manner that hadn't been there before.

Aristo shrugged. 'My mother's more of a hostess than a cook.'

He studied her face calmly. Last night she had not only acknowledged and accepted the irresistible sexual pull between them, but she had also shared her past with him, and he'd been hoping that if he could get her to drop her defences again then maybe, finally, she might consider sharing the future with him.

Only, judging by Teddie's cool demeanour this morning, she was still not ready to trust him completely. For a moment he considered giving her some space, but he had a responsibility to make this work, to make her see why it had to work.

'What are your plans for later?' he asked abruptly.

She glanced up at him, her eyes wide and clear. 'Nothing. The pool, probably—why?'

'Because I thought you and I might spend the afternoon together.' His dark gaze roamed her face. 'Just the two of us. There's something I want you to see...'

'You're sure that Melina is okay about this?'

Turning towards Teddie, Aristo picked up the hand that was clenched between her knees and squeezed it. It had taken some persuasion to convince her to leave their son back at the villa. Now that she was here, though, he was determined to let nothing interfere with his plans.

'I'm one hundred per cent sure,' he said firmly. 'You *are* allowed to have child-free time. Besides, Melina adores George, and he loves spending time with her—and if there's any problem we can be back in ten minutes. That's why we're taking the boat.'

Grinning, he gestured towards the front of the speedboat, where Dinos sat with one hand resting lightly on the wheel.

'And Dinos gets to go fishing without Melina getting on his case, so everyone's happy.'

Teddie shook her head, smiling back. 'I've never really understood fishing—it seems so boring.'

'It's not boring—it's shopping, but with a rod.'

His eyes gleamed and she punched him lightly on the arm. 'Clearly you've never been shopping.'

'Clearly you've never been fishing,' he countered.

Her eyes widened. 'And *you* have, I suppose?'

She felt a rush of heat as his gaze swept over her. 'Only once.'

He lowered his head, brushing his mouth against her cheek, his warm breath sending a flutter of sensation across her skin so that she felt a bite of hunger low down.

'But I was careless and I let her get away,' he whispered.

His head dipped and he kissed her mouth softly, his hands tangling in her hair, pulling her closer as the boat's engine slowed and then stopped.

Lifting his mouth, he glanced past her. 'We're here.' Turning towards her, he held out his hand. 'Come on—let's go see the rest of my island!'

It was more rugged at this end, Teddie decided as Aristo led her away from the beach and an extremely happy Dinos. Instead of being sandy, the beach was pebbled and the sea was a deep nautical blue.

The light was soft through the olive trees, but

as the path climbed upwards she soon started to feel breathless.

'Sorry!' Slowing his pace, he glanced down at her, his expression contrite.

Frowning, she stared at the olive grove. 'It didn't seem like a hill from down there.'

He grinned. 'It's not far now.'

She could hardly believe it was the first time she had left the villa since arriving. But it was hard to keep track of time on the island, and the days had blurred in a haze of eating, swimming and sleeping.

Although neither of them had slept much last night.

The thought popped into her head and this time the heat on her face had nothing to do with the sun.

'This is it.'

Aristo had stopped beside her and, turning with relief to where he was looking, she felt her heart-beat skip backwards as she stared down at the ruins of some kind of monument.

She breathed out softly.

'It's actually why I bought the island.'

He spoke quietly but she could hear the emotion in his voice.

'It's incredible.'

She shook her head, hardly able to take in what she was seeing. Juxtaposed against an impossibly turquoise sky, the pale stone columns looked fantastical, so that she half expected a centaur to step out from behind one.

'Can we get any closer?'

Nodding, he drew her against him, his hand sliding up her back as his mouth covered hers.

Heat flooded her and she could feel herself melting, her body softening against the hard breadth of his chest.

Breathing out unsteadily, he lifted his mouth, and stared down at her, his dark eyes gleaming. 'Is that close enough?'

Heart thudding, she gave him what she hoped was a casual smile and lightened her voice. 'I was talking about the ruins.'

'Come on, then.'

He caught her hand in his and they followed the sage-scented track down the hillside, past clumps of almost violently pink cistus.

Up close, the ruins were breathtaking. Standing in the shadow of the columns, it was impossible for her not to be impressed by their size—and the fact that they were still standing. But it wasn't just about size or age, she thought, gazing at them in silence. It was about the human cost of building it. How had they got the stone there? And how long had it taken for them to carve it with such precision?

His hand closed around hers and, turning to him, she smiled. 'Is it a temple?'

He nodded. 'To Ananke,' he said softly. 'God-dess of destiny and necessity. She's very important because she directed the fate of gods and mortals.'

He was kissing her as he spoke, feather-light but feverish kisses against her mouth and throat. She was losing concentration, losing herself in the feel of his lips on her skin.

Drawing back slightly, she frowned. 'I've never heard of her.'

'Shh!' He held up his finger to his lips, but he was smiling. 'I need to keep in her good books until after I've floated the business.'

Teddie glanced at him uncertainly. Why was he bringing up work now—here? It seemed al-most sacrilegious, not to say out of place, but the hazy sunshine was touching his dark eyes with gold and she felt dizzy with a longing that was al-most like vertigo.

'I thought it was hard work and a go-getting at-titude that built your empire,' she said teasingly.

His mouth curled upwards and he took a step closer, so that suddenly she was breathless with his nearness.

To hide the tangle of desire and excitement twisting inside her, she slipped free of his grip, stepping sideways and behind a pillar, darting out of reach as he followed her.

'You're not telling me you really believe in all that stuff about destiny?' she said, as he caught her wrist and spun her against him. Her pulse butter-flied forward as she felt his muscles tighten.

'I used to not,' he said slowly.

She swallowed. There was a tension in the air, a stillness and a silence, as if a storm was about to break, and she had to count the beats of her heart to steady herself.

'So what changed your mind?'

He lifted his head, and their gazes locked. 'You did. When you decided to meet Edward Claiborne in my hotel.'

She looked startled—and confused, Aristo thought as her green eyes widened.

'I don't understand.'

'That's okay. I didn't either. Not until we got here.'

He stared past her at the ruined temple, his pulse oscillating inside his head, wanting, needing to find the words that would make her change her mind—

'That first evening, when you and George went to bed, I was so tense I couldn't sleep. So I went out for a walk and I ended up here.' He frowned, remembering how he'd felt suddenly calm and res-olute as he'd wandered between the columns. 'I couldn't stop thinking about everything that's hap-pened. You being at the Kildare. Me going to your apartment. All of it so nearly didn't happen—and yet it did.'

Her hand tightened in his. 'I wasn't even supposed to be there. Elliot was. But he'd double-booked himself so I had to go instead,' she said quietly.

'That's exactly what I'm talking about. Don't you see, Teddie? You and me meeting again—it's fate. Every single thing that's happened could have gone a thousand different ways, but each time fate's pushed us closer. We're meant to be together...we belong to each other.'

Teddie blinked. She wanted to believe him, and he made it sound so compelling, so plausible, so certain. It was why she'd fallen in love with him.

Remembering those long late-night phone calls, she felt her pulse jump in her throat. But then Aristo had always been able been a good storyteller. Only, she already knew how their story would end.

Something of her thoughts must have shown on her face. Dropping her hand, he took a step closer and captured both her arms, tightening his hands around her shoulders.

'Are you happy?'

She looked up at him in confusion. 'What do you mean?'

'Are you happy? Here? With me?'

His words sent her stomach plunging, but even as she considered lying, she was nodding slowly. 'Yes, but—'

'But what?'

She frowned. 'But it's not that simple.'

'It could be,' he said fiercely. 'And I want it to be. I just need you to give our relationship a second chance. To give *me* a second chance so I can be the husband you deserve and the father George needs. I want you to marry me.'

She couldn't speak. She was too scared that she would agree to what he was asking—just as she'd done four years ago.

Her heart gave a thump.

She was scared too, of what would happen if she said yes. Their marriage might have lasted six months on paper, but even before their honeymoon had ended she had taken second place to his work. And now his empire was even bigger, his workload more demanding. How was he going to find the time for a wife *and* a child?

Wyatt had certainly never managed it, and she and her mother had just learned how to live with his absences. But she didn't want that for George. To know what he was missing but be powerless to change it.

Only, what would happen if they split up? How would George react? Having only just bonded with his father, he might choose to stay with Aristo. Would she lose her son as well this time?

The thought made her legs start to shake.

'George needs me.'

'Of course he does.' He sounded genuinely shocked. 'I would never take him away from you. You've done an incredible job, caring for him on your own for three years, but I don't want you do have to do it on your own any more. I want to be there for you—for both of you.'

'I can't marry you.' She pressed her hands against his chest until she felt him release his grip, and then he took a step backwards, giving her space. 'I'm sorry, Aristo, but I can't—I know it feels like things can work out between us, because I feel it too. But this isn't real life, and once we leave the island it won't be the same—you know that.'

Her throat felt as if it was lined with sandpaper.

'You and I—' she looked up at him, her eyes blurry with tears '—we are impossible.'

'Any more impossible than Elliot choosing to meet Claiborne at *my* hotel? Or you stepping in for him at the last moment?' His dark gaze was burning into her face. 'The impossible happens all the time, Teddie.'

She shook her head. 'You hurt me.'

The tremble in her voice seemed to belong to a completely different person. She hadn't meant to say it so bluntly, let alone out loud and to Aristo, and the shock of her admission silenced her.

'We hurt each other,' Aristo said after a pause. 'But we're not those people any more, so let's forget them and what happened then. Marry me and we can start again.'

Teddie stared at him in silence. It would be so easy to say yes. So much between them was good, and she knew how happy it would make George, and how miserable he was going to be if they returned home without Aristo. But how much worse would it be if his father was a full-time presence in his life?

She gave a small shake of her head. 'That's not going to happen, Aristo.'

Her voice was calm. Everything was so beautiful—the sunlight, the temple, the shimmering blue sea stretching away to the horizon, their new mood of intimacy and of course Aristo himself—and she didn't want to make it ugly with a stupid, pointless argument.

Nothing moved in his face. He held her gaze. 'We could make it happen.'

'But we don't need to.' She tried again to lighten the atmosphere between them. 'You asked me if I'm happy, and I am. We both are. So why add unnecessary complications?'

She could almost see him examining her words, deliberating and weighing up his response. Her heartbeat accelerated. His expression was one she recognised, for she'd seen it often, when he had been on the phone or at his laptop at their home, and it hurt that he was treating his ex-wife and child like some glitch at work.

Aristo frowned. He could sense her retreating from him—could feel their mood of easy intimacy starting to shift into something more strained—and even though he'd been the one to introduce the topic of marriage he felt irrationally angry with her.

'For someone claiming to want honesty and openness you're being a little disingenuous. Surely marriage would simplify matters between us. It will certainly simplify matters for George.'

Teddie stared at him in silence for a moment. 'How? By moving him away from the only home he's ever had to live in some uptown mausoleum? I told you before—he has friends, a routine, a life.'

'And now he has a father. Or am I less important than some random three-year-old he sits next to at lunch?' He shook his head dismissively. 'Kids change friends all the time at that age, Teddie.'

'I know that,' she said sharply. 'And, no, I don't think you're less important—just deluded. Listen to yourself! We bumped into one another in a hotel less than a week ago and now you want us to re-marry. I mean, who does that, Aristo?'

He kept his gaze hard and expressionless. 'We did. Four years ago. Okay, it was seven weeks, not one.'

'And look how that turned out!' She stared at him in disbelief. 'It was hardly a marriage made in heaven.'

Aristo steadied himself against the pillar. The script he'd prepared inside his head was unravelling—and faster than he could have imagined. *Focus*, he told himself. *Remember why you brought her here.*

'This time will be different. In six weeks I'm floating my business on the stock exchange. Leonidas Holdings will soon be a household name. I can give you and George everything you need, everything you've ever wanted.' Some of the tension left his muscles and he exhaled slowly. 'You could both come to the ceremony. They might even let George ring the bell.'

Teddie felt as though her legs were going to give way. She felt dizzy, misery and fury tangling with her breath. She'd thought they were talking about getting married, and yet somehow they'd ended up talking about his business. Even now, when he was proposing, she was somehow relegated to second place.

'So that's what this is about? Some photo op for the Leonidas empire.'

'No, of course not.'

'Why "of course not"?' she said shakily. 'Everything you do is ultimately about business.'

Uncoupling her eyes from his, she took a step backwards, her shoulders tensing, her slim arms held up in front of her chest like a boxer. Only, somehow the gesture made her look more vulnerable.

'We should never have married. Whatever happened in your bed last night doesn't change that, and it certainly doesn't mean we should marry again.'

'Teddie, please...'

'Can't you see? I don't have a choice.' She could feel the tears, and knew she couldn't stop them. 'There's no point in talking about this any more. I'm going to go back to the boat now.'

As she darted past him she heard him swear softly in Greek, but it was too late—she was already halfway up the path, and running.

CHAPTER EIGHT

SLAMMING HER BOOK SHUT, Teddie tossed it to the end of her bed.

It was a romantic novel, with a heroine she really liked and a hero she currently hated. She'd been trying to read for the last half-hour, but she couldn't seem to concentrate on the words. Other more vivid, more significant words kept ping-ponging from one side of her head to the other.

She could practically hear Aristo's voice, feel the intense, frustrated focus of his dark gaze, smell the scent he wore on her own skin—even though she'd showered, his phantom presence was still flooding her senses. Her heart was suddenly beating too fast.

The walk back to the boat had seemed never-ending. She had half expected him to follow her, if only to have the last word. Then she'd been scared that he'd wait and make his own way back, leaving her to somehow explain his absence to Dinos.

But she needn't have worried on either count. He had turned up perhaps five minutes after her and seamlessly picked up where he'd left off earlier in the day, engaging Dinos in conversation about his day's catch.

Back at the villa, their son's innocent chatter had

been a welcome distraction, but the whole time she'd been dreading the moment when they would be alone again.

Only, again she needn't have worried, for Aristo had politely excused himself after kissing George goodnight.

And she should have been pleased—grateful, even—that he had finally got the message. Instead, though, she had felt oddly disappointed and, lying here now, she still couldn't shift the sense of loss that had been threatening to overwhelm her since she'd turned and walked away from him at the temple.

Rolling on to her side, Teddie leaned over and switched off the light, reaching inside herself for a switch that might just as easily switch off her troubled thoughts.

But her brain stayed stubbornly alert.

Perhaps she should close the shutters.

Normally she only shut the muslin curtains, liking the way the pale pink early-morning light filtered softly through them at daybreak. But tonight the room felt both too large and yet claustrophobic, and she knew closing the shutters would only add to the darkness already inside her head.

Besides the temperature had risen vertiginously during the afternoon, and she wasn't prepared to shut out the occasional whisper of cool sea air.

It hardly seemed possible that only this morning

she had made peace with herself, accepting that the sexual longing she felt for Aristo was not shameful in any way, nor something she would come to regret. That it just *was* and there was no point in questioning it or fighting it.

But, although she was willing to give in to the temptation of a sexual relationship with Aristo, marriage was something she was going to continue resisting. She'd spent too long dealing with the chaos and devastation caused by the men in her life to let it happen again to her or her son.

Gazing at the moonlight through the curtains, she felt her heart contract. Maybe a fling wasn't what she would chosen if she could have had exactly what she wanted. But, as she'd already told him, she couldn't have that, and right now it was enough. All she wanted to do was live each minute as fully as possible until the inevitable moment of their separation when they returned to New York.

And it could have worked—only, typically of Aristo, he'd had to push for more—

Her stomach muscles tensed, frustration slicing through her. Nothing was ever good enough for him. He had a beautiful home in one of the most vibrant, exciting cities in the world, another in Athens, this mythically beautiful island and who knew how many other properties scattered across the globe? He owned a string of hotels and resorts and could probably retire now. But she knew he would never stop, that there would always be something driving him onwards, chasing him to the next goal.

Right now it was getting Teddie to marry him. And if she agreed to that then it would be something else.

Why couldn't he have left things as they were? Why couldn't he have just enjoyed the absence of complication in this new version of their old relationship? What was so wrong with allowing things to remain simple for just a few more days?

She didn't understand why he couldn't be satisfied, and she was tired of not understanding. Suddenly and intensely she wanted to talk to him.

Swinging out of bed, she snatched up a thin robe, pushing her arms into the sleeves as she walked determinedly across her bedroom. But when she reached the door she stopped, the rush of frustration and fury that had propelled her out of bed fading as quickly as it had arisen.

Did she really want to have this conversation now?

No. *Only, how could she not?*

Maybe he wasn't her husband any more, but she was going to have to deal with Aristo on a regular basis—and how would that ever work if she allowed the issue of remarrying to sit unquestioned, unanswered between them?

Knowing Aristo as she did, he wasn't going to

give up without a fight. So why not take the fight to him?

Heart thumping, she opened the door and walked purposefully out into the softly lit hallway. But before she had gone even a couple of paces her feet faltered and she came to an abrupt standstill, her pulse beating violently against her throat as though it was trying to leap to freedom.

Aristo was sitting on the floor, his long legs stretched out in front of him and blocking her way. As she stared down at him in stunned silence his dark gaze lifted to her face, and instantly she felt her shoulders stiffen and her heart begin to beat even faster.

'What are you doing?' she said hoarsely.

Holding her breath, she watched as he got to his feet in one smooth movement.

He shrugged. 'I couldn't sleep. So I got up to do some work, only I just couldn't seem to concentrate.' He looked up at her, his mouth curving crookedly. 'This may come as a surprise to you, but apparently everything isn't ultimately about business after all.'

She recognised her own words, but they sounded different when spoken by him. Less like an accusation, more self-deprecating. But even if that was true, she knew he was probably just trying a new tactic.

'So…what? You thought you'd stretch your legs

instead?' she said, glancing pointedly at his long limbs, her green eyes wide and challenging. 'What do you want, Aristo?'

His gaze didn't shift. 'I want to talk to you. I was going to knock on your door.'

'But you didn't.'

'Your light was off. I thought you must be asleep.'

She hesitated, then shook her head. 'I couldn't sleep either. Actually, I wanted to talk too. I was coming to find you.'

Aristo felt his chest tighten.

Watching Teddie practically sprint away from the temple, he'd had to summon up every atom of willpower to stop himself from chasing after her and *demanding* that she agree to what was clearly the only possible course of action open to them. Despite his frustration at the relentless circular dynamics of their relationship, and her stubborn, illogical opposition, he'd held back.

He'd felt too angry. Not the cold, disbelieving anger he'd felt four years ago, when he'd returned to their apartment to find her gone, or even the gnawing, twisting fury at learning he was father to a three-year-old he'd never met.

No, his anger had been hot and tangled with fear—an explicable fear, not new but still nameless—and that had angered him further because he couldn't control what he didn't understand. He'd known that he needed time to cool off, so he'd forced himself to stand and watch her disappear, to wait until his heart beat more steadily. And then back at the villa, he'd made himself turn in before her.

Of course he hadn't been able to sleep. His room still resonated with her presence from the night before. But even if it hadn't, he would have been incapable of thinking about anything but her.

And it wasn't just about the sex.

In a lot of ways that would have been easier, more straightforward. He gritted his teeth. But then nothing about Teddie was straightforward. She was an impossible to solve magic trick—thrilling and compelling and mystifying.

Look at her now. She might say she wanted to talk, but the expression on her face was an almost perfect hybrid of defiance and doubt, and he could sense that she was holding her body ready. Maybe ready to fight but, knowing Teddie, more likely ready to flee.

He felt the muscles of his face contract. He didn't want to fight with her any more, and he certainly didn't want to make her run.

Only, they couldn't just stand here in the darkness for ever.

'I don't want to force this…' He spoke carefully, willing her to hear his words as an invitation, not a trap. 'So I'm going to go downstairs and sit by the pool. If you want to join me that's great, and if not then I'll see you in the morning.'

Outside, the air was slightly cooler and he breathed in deeply, trying to calm the thundering of his heart. Had he said enough to reassure her that they could survive this conversation?

He wasn't sure, and as the silence stretched out into the night he was on the verge of turning and walking back into the villa. Then he saw her walking stiffly out onto the deck.

She stopped in front of him, close enough that he could see her eyes were the same colour as the wild pines that grew in the centre of the island, but not so close that she couldn't bolt back into the darkness.

'I don't want to argue,' he said after a moment.

She held his gaze. 'And you're saying I do?'

He held up his hands. 'No—that's not what I meant. Look, Teddie, I'm not looking for a fight. I'm just trying to fix this.'

'Fix what?' She glanced up at him, and then away into the darkness. 'Me? Us? Because I don't need fixing, thank you very much, and there is no us.'

'So what was last night about?'

'Last night was about sex, Aristo.'

'Not sex—passion,' he said softly.

'Whatever! It's just chemistry, pheromones.' She made her voice sound casual, even though her fingernails were digging into the palms of her hand. 'That's all.'

'That's all?' he repeated incredulously. 'You think last night was run of the mill?'

'No, of course not.' Her cheeks flushed. 'I'm not saying what we have isn't special. I know it is—that's why we've got this arrangement. So can't we just enjoy it? Do we have to keep talking about marriage?'

A muscle flickered in his jawline. 'Yes, we do. This "arrangement" works here, but it's not practical long-term.'

'Practical?' She took a deep breath. 'I thought we were talking about passion, not putting up some bookshelves.'

He gazed at her steadily, but she saw something flare in his dark eyes.

'So how do you see it working, then, Teddie? Is it going to be sex in the afternoons, when George is at school? Are we going to have to get up early and move beds every time one of us sleeps over?' His lip curled. 'But I'm guessing you don't even have a spare bed, so what will happen? Are you expecting me to sleep on the sofa?'

Her hands clenched into fists. 'That's the point. I'm not expecting anything. And you shouldn't expect anything from me—particularly marriage.'

She might as well not have spoken. Even as she watched him searching through that handsome head of his for some new line of attack he was already speaking.

'You told me you wanted us to be honest with one another.'

Heart pounding, she stared at him in mute frustration. 'So be honest! What you really want from me is sex, but you *need* me to be your wife because you want a wife.'

'Not just *a* wife. I want *you*.'

She shook her head. 'You don't want me—not really.'

'I know you don't believe that.'

'You don't know anything about me,' she snapped. She was starting to feel cornered, hemmed in by his refusal to see anything except from his own point of view. 'And what's more you don't want to know.'

Watching his jaw tighten, she knew that he was biting down on his temper.

'That's not true.'

'Yes, it is. You have this idea of what a wife should be, and I'm not it, Aristo.' She took a breath, trying to stay calm. 'Please don't bother trying to pretend I'm wrong. There's no point. I know I'm not enough. I've known that since I was five years old—'

She broke off, startled not just by the stunned look on Aristo's face but by the words she'd spoken out loud, for up until now her the subject of her father had always been a conversational no-go area.

'What are you talking about?' he said slowly.

She shook her head, not trusting herself to speak, frightened by what she might say next. 'It's nothing,' she said finally. 'Just a sad little story you don't want to hear.'

His heart in his mouth, fearful of losing her but more fearful of chasing her away, he watched her walk into the darkness, counting slowly to ten inside his head before following her.

She was sitting by the pool, head lowered, feet dangling into the water.

'I do want to hear it. I want to hear everything.'

The beams from the underwater lights lit up her fine features as though she was standing on a stage, about to perform a monologue—which she was, in a way, he thought, watching her slim shoulders rise and fall in time with her breathing.

There was a tight little pause, and then she said quietly, 'The first time my dad left I didn't miss him. I was too young—just a baby. He came back when I was about George's age, maybe a bit older.'

She lifted her face and his breathing stilled at the expression on her face. She looked just as he imagined she would have done as a little girl, just like George had looked when he'd told him that he was his father—solemn and shy, eyes wide with wonder.

'What happened?' He made himself ask the question but he already knew the answer. He could see it in the pulse beating savagely in her throat.

'He stayed long enough that I minded when he left, which was when I was about five. And then again when I was eight, then nine.'

She looked up at him briefly and he nodded, for he had no idea what to say.

'He was always chasing some get-rich-quick scheme, making promises he couldn't keep, borrowing money he couldn't pay back, gambling the money he did have on the horses. And sometimes he'd get out a pack of cards and teach me a trick. He was good—he probably could have made a career out of magic—but he liked taking risks and that's what he did when I was fourteen. He pretended to be a lawyer and got caught trying to con some widow out of her life savings.'

She looked away, and Aristo could tell that she was fighting to stay calm.

'I think he'd been lucky up until then. He was so handsome and charming he could usually get away with most things. But maybe his luck had run out or his charm couldn't hide all his lies any more. Anyway, he got sent to prison for eight years.'

Her eyes met his and she gave him a small, bleak smile that felt like a blade slicing into his skin.

This time he couldn't stay silent. 'I'm so sorry... I can't imagine what that must have been like for you.'

Nor had he ever tried. Of course he hadn't known the full story, but he had been too wrapped up in his own fears and doubts to consider it.

He'd sensed a wariness in her but, looking back, he knew that each time she'd hesitated he had simply ignored the signs and used his charm to convince her—just like he'd done in Vegas.

'Do you know what's the really sad part? Him being in prison was okay. It was actually better than how it was when he normally disappeared. You see, it was the first time I actually knew where he was. And he was pleased to see me, and that had hardly ever happened before. Usually he was distracted by some stupid scam.'

And then she'd met *him*, Aristo thought, swallowing, feeling shame burning his throat. A man who had brought her to a tall tower in a strange city, showered her with gifts and promises he hadn't known how to keep, then neglected her—not for some stupid scam, but for the infinitely more important and pressing business of building an empire.

No wonder she found it so difficult to trust. Her father had laid the foundations and he had unthinkingly reinforced her reasons to feel that way.

'I don't know how you survive something like that,' he said quietly. Except Teddie hadn't just survived. She'd faced insurmountable obstacles and triumphed.

She shrugged. 'It got worse before it got better. My mum lost it—big-time. I kept having to stay home to take care of her so my school got involved, and then I had to go and live with foster parents. Only, we weren't a good fit and I kept running away, so basically I ended up in care.'

Teddie swallowed. She couldn't look at him, not wanting to see the diffidence or, worse, the pity in his eyes.

'It wasn't all bad, though. That's where I met Elliot,' she said defiantly.

'Teddie...'

She tried to block the softness in his voice, but then she felt his hand on hers.

'Don't be nice to me.'

She pushed him away. If he touched her she would be lost, but he was taking her hand again, wrapping his fingers around hers, and she was leaning into him, closing her eyes against the tears.

'I don't want your pity.'

'Pity? I don't pity you.'

He lifted her chin and, looking into his fierce, narrowed gaze, she knew that he was telling the truth.

'I'm in awe of you.'

She bit her lip, stunned by his words. Four years ago she'd thought that hearing the truth would give him a bulletproof reason to walk away, and yet he was here, holding her close, his heartbeat beating in time to hers.

'I should have told you the truth before. But I thought you'd get bored with me before then.'

He shook his head, clearly baffled. 'Bored! Yeah, you're right—I can understand why you thought that might happen.' When she didn't respond, he frowned. 'Seriously?' he said softly. 'Don't you *know* how smitten I was?'

Her heart gave a thump; her eyes slid away from his. 'It was all so quick…and I guess you weren't really my type.'

His eyes looked directly into hers. 'You had a type?'

'Yes—no. I just meant the other men I dated weren't like you.'

Her cheeks felt hot. How could she explain his beauty, his aloofness, the compelling polished charm of a man born to achieve?

'They were scruffy guys I met in bars. You didn't even look at the bill before you paid it.'

The faint flush of colour on her cheeks as much as her words did something to soothe her remark about him not being her type, but he was still trying to understand why she thought he would have got bored with her.

There was a drawn-out silence. Teddie could feel the curiosity behind his gaze, but it was hard to shape her thoughts, much less articulate them out loud.

'It wasn't about you really—it was me. Even before we got married I felt like an imposter. And then when I moved into the apartment I panicked.

It felt like when I was child, with my dad. I just couldn't seem to hold you—you were so focused on work.'

'*Too* focused.'

He breathed out unsteadily, knowing now how difficult it would have been for her to admit how vulnerable she was—how difficult it must still be.

'You're an incredible person, Teddie, and your father was a fool not to see that. You deserved better than him.'

He brushed his lips against her forehead, the gentleness of his touch making her melt inside.

'You deserved better than me.'

Reaching up, she rested the back of her hand against the rough stubble of his cheek and his arm tightened around her.

'I never meant to hurt you,' he said. 'I just wanted it to be different with you.'

'Different from what?' she asked.

He frowned. It was the first time he'd ever spoken those words out loud. The first time he'd really acknowledged his half-realised thoughts to himself.

'From what I imagined, I suppose.'

She glanced down into the pool and then back up to his face, her expression suddenly intent. 'What *did* you imagine?'

He hesitated, his pulse accelerating, but then he remembered her quiet courage in revealing her own painful memories and suddenly it was easier to speak. 'My parents' marriage.'

Her green eyes were clear and gentle. 'I thought you said it was civilised?'

His mouth twisted. 'The divorce was civilised—mainly because they had nothing to do with it. But the marriage was positively toxic. Even as a child I knew my mother was deeply unsatisfied with my father, their friends, her home…'

He paused, and she felt the muscles in his arm tremble.

'And me,' he said.

Teddie swallowed. She felt as though she was sitting on quicksand. Aristo sounded so certain, but that couldn't be true. No mother would feel that way. But she knew that if she was upset George always worried that he'd done something wrong…

'She might have been unhappy, but I'm sure that didn't have anything to do with you. You're her son.'

He flexed his shoulders, as though trying to shift some weight, and then, turning, he gave her a small, tight smile. 'She has two sons, but she prefers the other one. The one who doesn't remind her of her mediocre first husband.'

Her hand fluttered against his face and she started to protest again, but he grabbed her fingers, stilling them.

'When I was five she moved out and took an apartment in the city. She left me behind. She said she needed space, but she'd already met Peter by then.'

Catching sight of Teddie's stunned expression, Aristo felt his throat tighten. But he had told her he was going to be honest, and that meant telling even the most painful truths.

'It's fine. I'm fine with it.' He stared down at the water and frowned. 'Well, maybe I'm not. I don't know any more.'

Teddie stared at him uncertainly. Her own mother had been hopeless, but she had never doubted her love—just her competence.

'But she must be so proud of you—of everything you've achieved. You've worked so hard.'

His profile was taut. He was still like a statue. 'Yes, I work. Unlike my half-brother, Oliver, who has a title and an estate. Not that it's *his* fault,' he added. 'It's just that her feelings were more obvious after he was born.'

His voice was matter-of-fact, but she could hear the hurt and her chest squeezed against the ache of misery lodged beneath her heart.

'But you like him?' she said quickly, trying to find something positive.

He shrugged. 'I don't really know him. He's seven years younger than me, and I was sent to boarding school when he was born. I guess I was jealous of him, of how much love my mother gave him. I've spent most of my life trying to earn that love.'

Her fingers gripped his so hard that it hurt, and he smiled stiffly.

'She left my father because she thought he wasn't good enough, and I guess I thought all women were like her—always wanting more, wanting the best possible version of life.'

'I never wanted that,' she said quietly.

The crickets were growing quieter now as the evening air cooled.

'I know. I know that *now*,' he corrected himself. 'But back then I suppose I was always waiting for you to leave me. When I came back from that trip after we argued about you giving up work, and you'd gone to see Elliot, I overreacted. I convinced myself that you were lying. That you didn't just want space.'

He could still remember how it had felt—that feeling of the connection between them starting to fade, like a radio station or mobile phone signal going out of range so that there would be periods when they seemed to skip whole segments of time and conversation. He'd been terrified, but it hadn't been only the sudden shifting insubstantiality of their relationship that had scared him, but the feeling that he was powerless to stop it.

'I did just want space.' She looked at him anxiously. 'I wasn't leaving you.'

'I *know*.' He pressed her hands between his. 'I'm to blame here. I was so convinced that you'd do what my mother did, and so desperate not to become my father, only I ended up creating the perfect conditions to make both those things happen.'

'Not on your own, you didn't!'

He almost smiled. 'Now who's being nice?'

She struggled free of his grip, clasping his arms tightly, stricken not just by the quiet, controlled pain in his voice but by what they had both pushed away four years ago.

'I was lonely and unhappy but I didn't address those problems—I didn't confront you. I ran away just like when I was a teenager.'

'I'd have run away from me too.' His face creased. 'I know I wasn't a good husband, and that I worked too hard, but it was difficult for me to give it up because work's been so important to me for so long. I didn't understand what it was doing to you—to us—but I've changed. I understand now, and you're what's important to me, Teddie—you and George.'

She wanted to believe him, and it would be so much easier to do so now, for she could see how her panicky behaviour must have appeared to him.

Last time the spectre of her parents' marriage—and his parents'—had always been there in the background. They'd both been too quick to judge the other. When the cracks had appeared he had overreacted and she had run away.

Her eyes were blurred with tears as she felt

barriers she had built long before they'd even met starting to crumble.

Maybe they could make it work. Maybe the past was reversible. And if they both chose to behave differently then maybe the outcome would be different too.

Aristo reached out and drew her closer and she splayed her fingers across his chest, feeling his heartbeat slamming against the palm of her hand.

'Please give me a second chance, Teddie. That's all I'm asking. I just want to put the past behind us and start again.'

His gaze was unwavering, and the intensity and certainty in his eyes made her heart race.

'I want that too,' she said hoarsely. 'But there's so much at stake if we get it wrong again.'

She thought about her son, and the simple life they'd shared for three years.

'I know,' he said softly. 'But that's why we won't get it wrong.'

If he could just get her to say yes…

She hesitated, her green eyes flickering over his face. He felt a first faint glimmer of hope, and had to hold himself back from pulling her into his arms and kissing her until she agreed.

'This time it will be good between us,' he said softly. 'I promise.'

Her head was spinning. It was what she wanted—what she'd always wanted. *He* was all she'd ever wanted, and she'd never stopped wanting him because she had never stopped loving him.

From the moment she'd chosen him to walk up onto that stage, his intense dark eyes and even darker suit teasing her with a promise of both passion and purpose, the world had been *his* world and her heart had belonged to him.

Her pulse fluttered. Around her there was a stillness, as though the momentousness of her realisation had stopped the crickets, and even the motion of the sea.

She searched his face. Could it be possible that Aristo felt the same way?

Looking up into his rigid, beautiful face, she knew that right now she wasn't ready to know the answer to that question, or even to ask it. She still hadn't replied to his marriage proposal—and, really, why was she waiting? She knew what she wanted, for deep down it was what she'd never stopped wanting.

'Yes, I'll marry you,' she said slowly, and then he was sliding his fingers through her hair, pulling her closer, kissing her deeply.

And there was only Aristo, his lips, his hands, and a completeness like no other.

CHAPTER NINE

SHIFTING AGAINST THE MATTRESS, Teddie blinked, opening her eyes straight into Aristo's steady gaze. It was the last morning of their holiday. Tomorrow they would be back in New York, and they would spend their first night as a family in what she thought of as the real world.

It was three days since she had agreed to become his wife—again—but even now just thinking about it made her breath swell in her throat.

She loved him so much—more, even, than she had before. Four years ago she had been captivated by his perfection. Now, though, it was his flaws that had enslaved her heart, the fact that he could feel insecure and trust her enough to admit it.

'What time is it?'

She stretched her arms slightly, her eyes fluttering down the line of fine dark hair on the smooth golden skin of his chest to where it disappeared beneath the crumpled white sheet. His hand slid over her stomach and she felt something shift and spiral down in her pelvis.

'What time do you want it to be?'

His finger was tracing the shape of her belly button, and suddenly she was struggling to speak.

'Early,' she whispered.

'Then you're in luck.' He gave her waist a gentle tug, pulling her closer so that she could feel the warmth radiating from his body.

Leaning forward, he kissed her softly, brushing his lips against her mouth, then down her throat and back to her mouth, and she pulled him closer, her fingers splaying over his shoulder as he stretched out over her.

He pushed inside her, gently at first, easing himself in inch by inch, then with more urgency. He breathed in sharply, his face taut with concentration, and she knew that he was having to hold himself back. She shivered, enjoying the power she had over him.

As though sensing her thoughts, he swore softly under his breath and then rolled over, taking her with him so that she was lying on top of him. Reaching up, he covered her breasts with his hands, playing with the nipples, feeling them harden, his dark eyes silently asking for and receiving her unspoken consent as he grasped her arms and pinned them against her body.

And then his mouth closed around her nipple, nipping and sucking at it fiercely, moving to the other breast until he felt her arching against him. He heard her gasp and, lifting his mouth, gazed up at her flushed cheeks, his dark eyes narrowed and glittering.

'You're so beautiful,' he murmured. 'I want to watch you.'

Teddie rocked against him. She could feel the impossibly hard press of his erection, could feel him growing thick, then thicker still, and she rocked faster, guiding his movement, wanting the merciless ache inside her to be satisfied.

Groaning, he let go of her arms, pulling her closer for more depth, driving into her until she began lunging forward, her whole body shaking as he tensed against her, his muscles clenching in one last breathless shudder.

Afterwards, they lay sprawled against one another, bodies damp and warm, fitting together with a symmetry that seemed to her as miraculous as any magic trick. The morning light was growing sharper, and soon they would have to get up, but for now it felt as though the beating of their hearts and the soft shadows at the edge of the room were holding back time.

Lifting her fingers, he flattened her hand against his. '"And palm to palm is holy palmers' kiss",' he said softly.

Tilting her head back, she looked up at him, her green eyes widening. 'Are you quoting Shakespeare?'

She felt her face grow hot and tight. Despite privately acknowledging her feelings for Aristo, something still restrained her from telling him that she loved him. Of course, she'd rationalised her behaviour, arguing to herself and to her conscience—in other words, Elliot—that the baseline of her love needed no public announcement or reciprocation.

Only occasionally did she wonder if it had more to do with a fear of how he would react.

Either way, it was getting harder to stay quiet—particularly if he added an ability to quote romantic lines to his armoury of charms.

He raised an eyebrow. 'Don't look so surprised. I don't just sit hunched over my laptop drooling over my bank balance. I have seen the occasional play.'

His fingers were lazily caressing her hip, and her breath caught as his lips brushed her collarbone. She leaned closer. He was so wonderfully sleek and warm, and the ceaseless rhythm of his fingertips was making it difficult for her to concentrate.

'So you like *Romeo and Juliet*?'

'Of course.'

His eyes gleamed, and she could hear the smile in his voice even before his mouth tugged upwards.

'Although I always thought there was scope for a sequel, where the paramedics arrive with an antidote.'

She held his gaze. 'You think they deserved a second chance at happiness?'

'Doesn't everyone?' He stared down at her intently, and she felt her pulse accelerate.

'That's not fair,' she said lightly. 'You can't quote Shakespeare and then look at me like that.'

Glancing down at her naked body, he groaned, and she felt him harden against the soft curve of her buttocks, felt her skin tighten in instant uncontrollable response.

'You're in no position to talk about fairness.'

Shifting forward, she slid her hand over his stomach. 'Who said anything about talking?'

Later, body aching, muscles warm and relaxed, she lay curled on her side, listening to the splash of water as Aristo showered. Outside, nothing was moving, and the faded crescent of last night's moon hung in the washed-out sky, a pale, fragmented twin for the blush-coloured sun that was starting its morning ascent.

She felt incredibly calm—and happy. There was hope now, where before there had been only doubt and fear and two damaged people circling one another. She knew Aristo now—not just as a lover but as a man. She knew where he came from, the journey he'd made to reach her, and he knew her journey too.

And from now on it would be *their* journey.

Her stomach flipped over as he walked back into the bedroom, a towel wrapped around his sleek, honed torso. His body looked as though it had been spray-painted bronze, and she lay breathless with heat and longing as he stood in front of the open doors, sunlight falling on his bare shoulders.

'Don't look at me like that,' he said without turning.

She blinked, her fingers clenching guiltily against the sheets. 'Like what?'

He walked towards her, and the single-minded focus in his dark eyes made a sharp, tugging current shoot through her.

He didn't answer, just dropped onto the bed beside her and leaned over, sliding his hands over her waist, pulling her body closer, kissing her, opening her mouth and, just like that, she was melting on the inside all over again.

Groaning, he lifted his mouth and rested his forehead against hers. 'You're not making this very easy for me...' he said softly. He shook his head. 'I can't believe we have to leave for New York this evening.'

Curling her fingers underneath the edge of his towel, she pulled him gently onto the bed beside her. 'Is that a problem?'

He sighed. 'I just want to stay here with you for ever.'

She rubbed her face against his cheek, then shifted against the pillows to meet his gaze. 'I want that too, but...'

'But what?' Reaching out, he ran his fingers through her hair, wrapping it around his hand, drawing her head back, letting his eyes roam hungrily over the length of her throat. 'We could easily stay a couple more days—a week, even.'

She stared at him, her head spinning. Did he even realise the full magnitude of his words? It wasn't just that he was offering to stay on the island but that he was prepared to neglect his business to do so.

Her heart was thumping. She'd been trying to ignore it, but their imminent return to reality had been ticking away in the back of her mind like a timed explosion, waiting to go off.

For the last few days she had been sublimely happy. They'd hardly spent a moment apart, and Aristo had never been more attentive, but part of her hadn't been able to help but wonder if that would change when the plane touched down in New York. If his promise of change would disappear along with the sand in their shoes.

Now, though, she realised that—incredibly—he had meant what he'd said, for he had just given her the proof she'd been subconsciously seeking that she didn't need to measure her happiness in days or weeks any more.

'We could…'

Sitting back, he studied her face assessingly. 'You're turning me down?'

Green eyes flaring, she nudged him with her

foot. 'I don't want to wear you out. I mean, you're not as young as you used to be—'

She broke off, yelping as he grabbed her foot and jerked her towards him, his dark eyes gleaming with amusement.

'Is that right?'

His fingers began sliding up her legs, over her ankles, moving lazily over her skin, and she breathed out unsteadily, feeling her body tighten in response.

'Of course I want to stay...'

She hesitated. Her job had always been such a contentious issue between them, but she couldn't run away this time. More importantly, she didn't want to.

'But I've got opening night at the Castine on Saturday. I have to be there.'

She wondered how he would respond to her putting *her* job first, but his eyes were impossible to read.

There was a short silence, and then, leaning forward, he kissed her gently. 'Then we'll be there.'

For a moment she didn't register his choice of words, and then suddenly she realised what he'd said.

Taking a breath, she said tentatively, 'I didn't know you were planning on coming.'

His gaze was steady and unblinking. 'I wouldn't miss it for anything.'

And, tugging her body towards him, he lowered his mouth and deepened the kiss.

The next two days fell into a pattern. They woke early, then made love until the morning light grew bright enough to wake their son. They had their meals on the terrace, swapping between the pool and the beach as the sun rose. Then, after George had gone to sleep, they retreated to Aristo's bedroom where they stripped one another naked, making love until they fell asleep.

It was the hottest day today, and they had gone to the beach in search of a breeze.

Stretching out her legs, Teddie gazed up at the cloudless sky. 'I forgot to tell you—Elliot texted me.'

Aristo frowned. 'Is there a problem?'

He watched as she glanced across to where George was jumping over the tiny waves that were undulating across the pale sand. Her uncomplicated connection with their son was still a source of wonder and joy to him. As was the new easiness between them.

She shook her head. 'No, it's good news. Apparently Edward's invited a whole bunch of his celebrity friends to come to the opening night. There's a tennis player, some actors, and that singer who sang at the Super Bowl—I can't remember her name.'

Picking up her hand, Aristo kissed it. 'It doesn't matter. They're going to love you.'

Teddie smiled automatically. *But not as much as I love you.*

Her heart beat faster as he leaned forward and brushed a few grains of sand from her arm, apparently unmoved by her words.

Unsurprisingly, as they'd been inside her head.

She glanced up at him, and then quickly away. Why was she being so spineless about this? It was the perfect opportunity to tell him the truth, but the words stayed stubbornly in her throat as he laced his fingers with hers.

'Of course they probably won't all turn up.' She smiled.

'They will. And I'll be there too,' he whispered, nuzzling her neck, his warm breath making her pulse jump.

'Thank you for doing this.' She gave his hand a quick squeeze. 'You'll probably find it insanely dull as you already know all my tricks.'

His eyes gleamed. 'Not *all* of them,' he softly. 'If last night was anything to go by.'

He had never felt so relaxed. No—not just relaxed, he thought reflectively. He felt liberated. Not only had he won Teddie back, he hadn't thought about work for days. Of course he was checking his email, once in the morning and once again in the evening, but the project he'd been working towards for years no longer seemed quite as important as the woman sitting beside him and their son.

How could anything compete with getting to know George and sharing his bed with Teddie?

He glanced down at their hands, at the way her fingers were entwined with his. And it wasn't just about sex. He wanted to hear her laugh, to *make* her laugh. He wanted to watch her fix her hair into that complicated bun thing that seemed to defy gravity. To hear her mischievous voice as she pretended to be the lonely giraffe in George's favourite bedtime story.

Four years ago he'd always had a sense that she was holding herself back, and he'd mistakenly assumed it was because she wasn't committed to him. Now, though, she had admitted the truth about her past. He had gained her trust. And that knowledge was an aphrodisiac more potent than any sexual act.

He looked up as, pulling her hand free, she nipped his arm with her fingers.

'You're about to be taken off the guest list,' she said threateningly, but she was laughing.

He grinned. 'Wouldn't matter. It's your big night. Whatever happens, I'm going to be there in the front row—that's a promise.'

She leaned against him. 'I can't believe it's happening.'

She couldn't. Nor that Aristo was going to be

there. It was a touching sign of his commitment both to her *and* her career. And yet another reason to reveal the depth of her feelings.

But right now she needed to concentrate on her upcoming show. She never got stage fright on the night, but in the days running up to a performance her nerves always got the better of her. And she hadn't so much as picked up a deck of cards for nearly two weeks.

Thankfully she'd brought a couple of packs with her, and now, leaving George and Aristo building an elaborate fortress out of sand on the beach, she returned to the villa and worked her way through her repertoire of tricks, some of which had taken five years to perfect.

As usual, she lost track of time, and it was only when she heard the sound of Dinos's motorboat, returning from its morning trip to the market, that she realised how long she'd been practising.

Packing away her cards, she ran quickly through the villa, down to the beach.

'Sorry,' she said breathlessly. 'I didn't realise how late it was.'

'Look what we built, Mommy!'

Grabbing Teddie by the hand, George hauled her over to where Aristo stood grinning beside a huge sandcastle.

'Wow! That's amazing! I think that is the best sandcastle I've ever seen.'

Eyes dancing, she stood on tiptoe and kissed Aristo softly on the mouth.

'And the biggest!'

Drawing her closer, he laughed.

'Daddy, can you take a picture?'

'Yes, of course he can, darling.' Teddie glanced down at her son. 'Do you want to be in it?'

Pulling out his phone, Aristo took a step backwards.

'Okay—hold your spade up, George.'

Aristo held his arm above his eyes to shield them from the sun, and was just starting to crouch down when his phone vibrated.

'Hang on a minute...' Glancing down at the screen, he frowned. 'I'm going to have to take this.'

Teddie watched in confusion as he held the phone up to his ear.

'What?' he said tersely. 'Well, can you explain to me why that's even happening?'

Without even looking back, he began walking away.

'Mommy?' George was standing beside her, staring uncertainly after his father. 'Where's Daddy going?'

'He's just got to talk to somebody. He'll be back in a couple of minutes,' she said quickly.

But five minutes later Aristo was still talking.

As Teddie tried to distract their son she could see Aristo out of the corner of her eye, pacing in circles, still talking, his shoulders braced.

It was obvious the call was work-related and, judging by the palpable frustration in his voice, there was some kind of problem—but was it really that urgent?

After another five minutes she took a reluctant George back up to the villa, having promised that Daddy would definitely not forget to take a photo of his sandcastle.

Standing in the living room, she gazed down at the beach, feeling her frustration starting to rise. But Aristo was the CEO of a huge global company, and she couldn't really begrudge him one phone call, no matter how long-winded. She was just lucky to have Elliot at home, fielding any potential work problems for her.

She glanced down to where Aristo was still pacing across the sand. It was obviously not a happy conversation, but a cup of his favourite *sketos* coffee would help restore his mood.

She was just about to head off to the kitchen when she saw him heading up the steps from the beach, moving fast, the phone still pressed his ears.

'I agree. I can't see a way round it. Okay. Thanks, Mike. We'll speak on the flight.'

Striding past her into the room, he tossed his phone onto one of the sofas. His jaw was tense, the skin of his face stretched taut across his cheekbones and, her heart hammering against her ribs, she stood in silence, feeling invisible, extraneous, frozen out.

'Is everything okay?'

He turned and stared at her blankly, almost as if he didn't know who she was, and then, frowning, he shook his head. 'No, it's not.' His eyes narrowed and he ran his hand over his jawline. 'But it's my own fault. This is what happens when I go off-grid.'

'What's happened?'

The air around him seemed to vibrate with tension.

'There's a problem in Dubai. For some incomprehensible reason they've been using single-use bottles out there and I need them replaced.'

Was that all? She felt a rush of relief. 'It's obviously just a mistake. Surely all you have to do is get someone to replace them?'

He stared at her impatiently.

'This isn't just about replacing bottles, Teddie. Leonidas hotels and resorts are supposed to be eco-friendly. If this gets out it's going to look like I'm greenwashing my business, and I can't have publicity like that—particularly when I'm about to float the company.'

Glancing down at his swim-shorts, he grimaced.

'I need to change,' he muttered and, turning, he began walking purposefully towards the stairs.

Change? She followed him, feeling slightly off balance.

'Are we going somewhere?'

He stopped, one foot on the first step, and to her agitated mind, he looked ominously like a sprinter waiting for the starter gun to be fired.

'Not we.' Turning, he locked his eyes with hers.

'I don't—'

'You don't need to go anywhere.'

Finishing her sentence, he smiled politely and she had a rush of *déjà-vu*—a familiar unsettling sensation of being demoted to 'any other business'.

'Look, this shouldn't take more than a couple of days,' he said calmly. 'Melina and Dinos will take care of you while I'm away.'

She felt a head-rush, his words pulling the blood away from her heart.

'What? You're going to Dubai?' Her legs felt flimsy suddenly, and she reached out to grip the bannister. '*Now?* Can't you send someone else?'

He stared past her, his features hard and closed. He could see the confusion in her eyes, and the disappointment in her clenched fists, and it hurt knowing that he was the cause, but he couldn't risk handing this over to someone else.

'Of course not. I need to be on the ground. I'll need to talk to the staff, and if anything's leaked out then I'll need to talk to the media. Otherwise it'll look as though I don't care about the promises I make.'

'*Promises?*'

Her grip against the bannister tightened. There was an ache inside her chest, cold and dark and heavy, spreading like an ink stain. 'What about the promises you made to *me*?' she heard herself saying.

His eyes didn't so much as flicker. 'Teddie, this is important. Otherwise—'

She cut him off. 'You said I was important to you,' she said flatly. 'You promised me that this time it was going to be good between us. You promised that you'd be at the opening of the Castine. In the front row.'

He frowned. 'And I will be—'

'How?' She interrupted him again. 'The opening show is on Saturday. Did you forget? Or maybe you just don't care.'

He said nothing and the chill seemed to spread to her limbs.

Aristo stared at her in silence. Her accusations stung—primarily because he couldn't deny them. He hadn't forgotten about her show, but he'd downgraded its importance—obviously, how could he not have done? There were always going to be other shows, but if he didn't go to Dubai then he would be jeopardising everything.

'Of course I care. That's why I'm going to Dubai.' His face felt so rigid with tension that it hurt to speak. 'Look, I don't want to leave you—'

'So don't!' Her eyes were fierce, the green blazing like the Aurora Borealis. 'Stay here with us—that's what you said you wanted.'

He stared at her, their conversation washing over him like the waves outside, pulling him in and drawing him away all at the same time.

He didn't want to leave her, but they couldn't stay here for ever, and this happening now was a reminder of what was at stake back in the real world—what he risked losing. Teddie might have told him that she didn't care about money and status, and he believed her, but now that she'd agreed to marry him he was determined that this time it would be perfect.

And if things got out of hand in Dubai then that wouldn't happen.

Glancing over, he saw that her eyes were too bright, but he let his anger block the misery twisting in his throat. He hadn't planned any of this, and he had no choice but to fix it in person. So why was she making it so hard? Just for once couldn't she just give him her unconditional support?

Reaching out, he took both her hands and, gripping them tightly, pulled her closer. 'Of course I care. Look, it's just one show. And I wouldn't be going to Dubai if there was any other option. But I can't risk the damage it will do to my reputation.'

Nor the knock-on consequences that damage would have when he came to issue a share price—because that was his goal. Then he would be able to join the business elite and leave his rivals in the dust.

That was his priority, in his role as husband and father.

Teddie swallowed past the lump in her throat.

She didn't recognise the man standing in front of her. Had he really just spent hours building a sandcastle with their son? Looking down at his hands, she felt her heart contract. She could feel his pulse beating frantically, urgently through his fingertips, and suddenly she understood.

This wasn't about some mess in Dubai, or his business reputation, this was about a childhood spent trying to win the love of his mother. And now he was trying to do the same with her and George. To earn their love.

That was why work mattered so much to him and why he wanted his name to be indelible.

But what would happen if he found out he was already loved? Unconditionally. Now and for ever. Maybe she could quiet the urgency inside him.

'I don't want you to go,' she said softly. Looking up into his eyes, she smiled unsteadily. 'And you don't need to go. If you don't ever float your business, whatever that means, it won't change how I feel about you, or how George feels about you.'

She cleared her throat.

'I love you, Aristo.'

Silence.

His dark eyes rested on her face and then, lifting her hands to his mouth, he kissed first one and then the other gently.

'I can't do this now.'

His voice was quiet, careful, almost as though he was scared of breaking something.

She stared at him, her heartbeat slowing. She'd never told anyone she loved them before—not even Aristo. Other phrases of love, maybe, but not those three specific words. But she knew that the correct response wasn't, *'I can't do this now.'*

'Is that all you're going to say?' she said shakily. 'I just told you I love you…'

'I can't, Teddie.' He let go of her hands.

Her chest was too tight, and then she felt her veins flood with shock and misery as she realised that what he'd been scared of breaking was *her*.

She opened her mouth to speak, but no words came out. She'd thought she knew what heartbreak felt like but she'd been wrong.

'I'm sorry,' he said stiffly. 'I really need to change. We can talk properly when—'

Her body felt numb, and it took an effort to shake her head. 'There's nothing to talk about.'

What was there to say? That she had stupidly fallen in love with a man who saw marriage as a means of tying up loose ends? She wasn't even going to try and deny the sexual chemistry between them, but everyone knew that passion burnt itself out. And if she hadn't been the mother of the heir to the Leonidas empire their relationship would no doubt have ended when they'd finally satisfied their hunger for one another.

He frowned. 'We'll talk when I get back. If you don't want to stay here, then go to the apartment. I'll make arrangements.'

'There's no need.' She was striving for calm. This wasn't going to turn into some slanging match. At least then this trip would be a happy memory for George. 'We won't be moving into the apartment. I'm not going to marry you, Aristo.'

His eyes narrowed. She could feel his disbelief, his frustration.

'Because I'm flying to Dubai? Don't you think you're overreacting a little?'

Time seemed to wind back four years, and suddenly it was as though they were back in the bedroom of that tall tower in New York, when he'd told he was going on yet another business trip.

She shook her head. 'No, I don't. This isn't about you flying to Dubai, it's about us being honest— or did you forget that too?'

He didn't respond, but his jaw tightened. 'I have been honest. I didn't plan this mess, and I can't just delegate it to someone else.'

He looked so serious, and so very beautiful, and she loved him so much, but it wasn't enough to make her turn a blind eye like her mother had done.

She knew Aristo was telling the truth—only they were small, inconsequential truths. She needed security in her and George's life, the emotional not the financial kind, and there was nothing to be gained by avoiding the bigger, uglier truths.

She took a deep breath. 'Just tell me the truth. Would you honestly have asked me to marry you if I hadn't had George?'

He glanced away, and in that small gesture she knew that it was over.

Her face didn't change. 'You should change, and then we need to tell George you're leaving.'

Silently, she willed him to look at her, but after a moment he turned and began walking upstairs.

CHAPTER TEN

TAKING A DEEP BREATH, Teddie closed the door to her wardrobe and gazed at her reflection in the mirror.

It was the first time she had been able to look at herself since getting back from Greece. Up until now she'd been too hollowed out with misery and despair to face the red-eyed proof of her failure, but tonight she had no choice.

Tonight was the opening night of the Castine, and she was going to be up on stage in front of the fifty personally invited guests of Edward Claiborne. Getting to this moment had been brutal, and the pain had been like nothing she'd ever experienced. But tonight was her night—hers and Elliot's—and she wasn't going to let herself or him down.

Turning slowly, she glanced over her shoulder. The jumpsuit was black…fitted. The top was guipure lace, long-sleeved, buttoning up the front to a high collar. The trousers were plain except for the long fringe that was really only visible when she moved.

Spinning round on her towering heels, she stared at herself critically, pressing her hand flat against her stomach in an effort to calm the jumping jacks twitching inside her.

She looked serious but that was okay. Perhaps a little intimidating. But that was okay too. An audience should have a healthy respect for magic, not see it as some kind of sideshow at a kids' party.

And it was a beautiful jumpsuit. Too expensive, of course, but she would be earning real money now, and for the past few days she had been uncharacteristically reckless in her spending. She'd given Elliot a new evening suit, as a thank-you for looking after the business, and she'd been lavishing George with presents too.

Her throat tightened. Not to say thank-you to him, but sorry. Sorry for giving his stupid, selfish father a second chance.

As soon as she'd seen Aristo in the lounge at the Kildare she should have walked straight past him and into a lawyer's office. Instead she'd not only let him back into her bed, but into her heart, had even agreed to marry him.

Her mouth trembled. She could forgive herself for falling into his arms. Given the sexual pull between them, it had been inevitable. But she had no excuse for falling in love with him again.

Breathing out unsteadily, she closed the wardrobe door.

She'd always been so concerned about not turning into her mother, but maybe she was actually more like her father, for she had let herself be seduced by daydreams instead of seeing the reality. And, just like Wyatt, she'd stupidly believed she could beat the house.

Gazing at her reflection, she let her hand drop.

One small mercy was that, thanks to some last vestige of self-preservation or common sense, she hadn't told George that she and Aristo were getting married. But she'd still had to explain to their overtired and confused son why they weren't going to Daddy's apartment.

She blinked back tears as she remembered their journey back from Greece.

When Aristo had left the island George had been moderately upset. But he'd assumed that they would be staying there until his father returned. It had only been when Teddie had told him that they were going back to New York without Aristo that he'd got hysterical.

She hadn't wanted to lie, and the truth was that she didn't know when—*if*—George would see his father again, but she had told him how much Aristo loved him, how much *she* loved him, and just saying the words had made her feel more confident. Whatever happened, she would be there for her son.

Her stomach clenched and she felt suddenly sick. She wished that she hadn't actually thought of Aristo by name. Ever since she'd got back home she'd been trying not to do so, even in her head. It just seemed to make her feel so much worse, and right now she didn't want to feel anything.

George had been inconsolable, refusing to leave Melina and then crying himself to sleep on the plane. Then and only then had she allowed her own tears to fall.

Thankfully, Elliot had been waiting outside her apartment. Opening the door of the taxi, he'd pulled her into a bear hug with one arm, scooped George into the other. He'd taken charge of everything—paying the driver, carrying in the suitcases and then ordering pizza.

He hadn't cross-examined her, but then he hadn't had to ask anything. He knew her well enough to see the pain behind her careful smile as she'd cut the pizza into triangles.

George had calmed down, but she was still worried about him. He hadn't slept in his own bed since they'd got back, and he seemed quieter than usual. Thankfully he loved his babysitter, Judith—a retired pre-school teacher and grandmother of twelve—so at least she wouldn't have to worry about leaving him tonight.

She heard the doorbell ring and instantly froze, her heart hammering against her ribs. But of course it was only Elliot's voice drifting through the apartment.

'Teddie?'

She took a breath. 'I'll be right there,' she called, knowing that she was wasting her time. He would see right through the over-bright note in her voice.

She felt suddenly guilty and stupid for wishing that it was Aristo waiting patiently in the living room for her to emerge instead of her friend—her good, loyal friend.

Guilty because Elliot deserved better, and stupid because right now she had no reason to believe that she would ever see Aristo again, given that he hadn't so much as texted her once.

Her mouth trembled and, feeling the threat of tears, she picked up her bag and walked quickly across her bedroom. She'd promised herself that tonight she was not going to cry any more tears for Aristotle Leonidas until the show was over.

And that was what was going to happen, for—unlike her ex—she actually kept her promises.

'You okay, babe?'

Edward Claiborne had sent a limo to collect them and, glancing across its luxurious interior, Teddie saw that Elliot's face was soft with worry.

She nodded. 'I will be.' She gave him a small crooked smile. 'And this evening will help, you know—being up there. I'll forget everything but the cards.'

Maybe she might even forget her shattered heart.

'I know.' He grinned. 'And I know I'm your

buddy, and that makes me not really a guy, but I gotta say you look smoking hot tonight, Teds!'

She managed a real smile then. 'You look good too, Els.'

The limo was slowing, and she could see the doorman stepping forward to greet the car. Her pulse started to accelerate. They had arrived.

Elliot held her gaze. 'You ready?' he said quietly, holding out his hand.

Nodding, she reached out to take it as the door swung open.

The Castine was the perfect setting for a magic show. There was no sign outside the door, and it was situated in a side street far away from the hustle of the city. On the first floor there was a bar and dining room, and on the second a jewel-coloured lounge that, despite its size, offered both intimacy and drama.

She could hear the buzz of people talking and the clink of glasses beneath the beating of her heart, and as she stepped under the spotlight she knew that all eyes were on her.

They just weren't his eyes.

And, despite knowing it was pointless, she still couldn't stop herself from quickly scanning the front row, unable to quell one last tiny hope that he would be there.

Of course he wasn't.

But they were an easy crowd to please—and not

just because of the waiters discreetly circulating the room with bottles of *prestige cuvée* champagne. Clearly, like their host, they appreciated magic, and as their applause filled her head she was finally able to admit what she had been fighting so hard to deny. She missed Aristo. Missed him so much that words were simply not adequate to describe the sense of loss, the loneliness, the aching bruise of his absence.

She already knew that she would never again share that dizzying chemistry with a man. But, together with their son, it was something nobody could ever take away from her—it would always be there inside her. And now, looking out into the blur of faces, she felt a tingling heat run down her spine, for she could almost feel him there in the audience, a shadow memory of that first time they'd met.

Two hours later it was over.

'Teddie, that was marvellous.' Edward Claiborne was the first to offer his congratulations. 'I honestly think she's a genius, don't you, Elliot?' He massaged his forehead. 'I've watched a lot of very talented magicians in my time, but with you I find it impossible to separate technique from performance. When you're doing a trick, I know something's happening but I just don't see it.'

'Well, he's happy,' Elliot said softly as they watched him shaking hands with an Oscar-winning actress. 'And he has some great connections.' He grinned. 'Hollywood, here we come!'

She punched him lightly on the arm. 'Hollywood is in California. You hate California, remember? That's why you moved to New York. Besides, it's hardly convenient for George's nursery.'

She made her way slowly back to the dressing room. In some ways the evening had been a triumph, but it had been a bittersweet triumph, for she knew now that no amount of applause and admiration would ever make her feel as complete as lying in Aristo's arms.

But there was no point in thinking about that now. *This is supposed to be your night, remember*, she told herself. And, taking a deep, cleansing breath, she walked into her dressing room.

And stopped.

Aristo was sitting on a chair, his head bowed, what looked like a phone clamped between his hands. As she took a faltering step backwards, her fingers gripping the door frame for support, he looked up, his dark eyes fixing on her face.

'Aristo.'

He was wearing a dark suit, and it was a shock seeing him dressed so formally, but of course this was real life now, and that meant work. Her stomach clenched as he stood up, but she forced herself to hold his gaze.

'Hello, Teddie.'

She stared at him in disbelief, trying to ignore the pain ripping through her chest. 'What are you doing here?'

Her arms had lifted to cross automatically in front of her body, and she willed her legs to stay upright.

'I came back for the show,' he said quietly. 'I told you I wouldn't miss it for anything.'

Her heart thumped inside her chest. 'Except you did. It just finished. But it doesn't matter.'

Her voice sounded wrong, too high and breathless, and she knew it didn't match her careless words, but she was past caring what he thought of her.

'You had something more important to do. You had to fix a crisis in Dubai.'

He shook his head. 'There was no crisis in Dubai.' His mouth twisted. 'Only, I'm such an idiot I had to go all the way there to work that out.'

'I thought you had to be there to talk to your staff and the media.'

Staring down into her eyes, he let out a long breath. 'I was wrong. I realised the only person I needed to talk to, the only person I *wanted* to talk to, was you. That's why I flew back to New York.'

He ran his hand across the face, and with a jolt she realised that although he was dressed in a suit, he looked nothing like the suave businessman who had left her on the island. His shirt was creased, and his unshaven face looked paler than usual, and he was actually holding his passport, not his phone.

He must have come straight from the airport and he must be exhausted. The two thoughts collided inside her head.

But, remembering how he'd let go of her hands when she'd told him she loved him, she pushed the thought away.

'Well, I'm sorry you had a wasted trip,' she said stiffly. 'Two wasted trips.'

'Teddie, please—'

'No, Aristo. I don't want to do this.' She shook her head. Her whole body was shaking now. 'If you want to see George, then talk to my lawyer.'

'I don't want to talk to your lawyer. I want to talk to you.'

He took a step forward, and even if she hadn't heard the strain in his voice she would have seen it around his eyes.

'I made you a promise. I said I'd be here, and I was. I know I wasn't in the front row. I got here too late for that. But I was at the back the whole time.'

She stared at him, blinking, remembering that moment when she'd felt his presence, how she'd thought it was just a phantom memory of the first time they'd met.

'I should never have left you. I knew I was making a mistake, but...' He paused, then frowned. 'But when you told me you loved me I panicked.'

His choice of words felt like a slap to the face. Could he make it any plainer that her feelings were not reciprocated? Her heart was a lead weight in her chest and she felt suddenly brutally tired.

'I don't need to hear this, Aristo,' she said flatly. 'I just want to go home.'

He shook his head. 'Not until you understand.'

Reaching out, he took hold of her arms, but she shook him off.

'I do understand. You don't love me and you only wanted to marry me because of George. I get it, okay? And now I want to go home.'

'Your home is with *me*, Teddie. And not just because of George.'

She started to shake her head, but he took her face between his hands and this time she didn't pull away.

'Look at me,' he said softly.

At first she resisted, but finally she lifted her chin.

'Maybe it was true at first, but not any more. George is our son, but he's not the reason I want to marry you. I want you to be my wife because I love you.'

'If you love someone you don't panic when she tells you she feels the same,' she said stubbornly.

He shook his head, his dark eyes narrowing. 'Not true. I love you, Teddie. And I did panic. As soon as you said those words I couldn't think straight. I just knew that I couldn't let anything mess up my business, the sale of the shares.'

'But I told you I don't care about any of that.'

He nodded. 'I know you don't—but I did. Look, I know it sounds crazy, but I've been chasing perfection all my life—first at school, then with work. And each time I reached my goal I'd set myself a new one.'

He frowned, as though baffled by what he was saying.

'When you told me you loved me I couldn't just say the words back to you. I wanted to *show* you how much I love you, and I thought that meant fixing things in Dubai, that if I couldn't do that then I didn't deserve to win you back. I was so desperate to make that happen, and so scared that it wouldn't. But as soon I got there I realised that I wasn't fixing anything, only breaking *us*, and that's why I came back to New York—'

His voice cracked, and he breathed out unsteadily.

'Because I can't lose you again, Teddie. The business, my career—none of that matters if we're not together. That's all I want...to be with you.' He stopped, his dark eyes on hers. 'If you'll have me. Do you think that's possible?'

Her heart was fluttering against her ribs, but her love for him felt solid and unbreakable. 'I do,' she said softly. Holding her breath, she searched his face, saw hope and love shining in his eyes.

He pulled her closer, wrapping his arms around her, burying his face against her hair. 'I thought I'd broken us.'

She felt his grip tighten.

'I was so scared that I'd ruined it, that I'd lost you.'

'You can't lose me. You're my husband, my heart.' Lifting her face, she smiled weakly. 'But if you'd told me you were coming I'd have saved you a seat.'

He loosened his grip. 'I think I left my phone on the plane.'

She looked up at him. 'What about Dubai?'

'I don't know.' He frowned, then slowly began to smile. 'And what's more I don't care. I really don't.'

'I need to sit down,' she said shakily.

He led her into the dressing room and pulled her onto his lap, his arms curving around her body so tightly that she could feel his heart beating in time to hers.

'You're an incredible magician, Teddie.'

Leaning back into his chest, she felt her face grow warm. 'Thank you. It went really well. But Elliot and I are definitely going to have to find some other acts to keep it fresh. Maybe a hypnotist—people always love watching that.'

'Maybe I could have a go. I've been practising a trick.'

His eyes were warm and steady on her face.

'You have?'

'You can never have too much magic in your life.'

His gaze drifted slowly over her face and she felt her pulse start to accelerate.

'Well, you can certainly audition.'

'Right now?'

'Okay.' She laughed. 'Do you have a stage name?'

He shook his head. 'I don't think I'm going to need one. It's going to be a one-off performance.'

She smiled. 'So what trick are you going to do?'

'It's one I made up myself.'

His face was soft and unguarded and she stared at him, transfixed by the glitter in his dark gaze.

'It's called the reverse disappearing ring.'

'Do you want me to tell you when to start?'

His eyes locked onto hers and she felt her blood lighten as he shook his head.

'No need. I'm done.'

She frowned, and then as he lifted her hand she felt her heart open up as she gazed down at the beautiful emerald ring on her finger.

'It was a bit last-minute in Vegas,' he said hoarsely. 'But I wanted to do it right this time.'

'I love it,' she whispered, her eyes filling with tears. 'And I love you.'

'I love you too.' Dipping his head, he kissed her gently. 'More than I ever believed I could love anyone. So much more. And it's going to be so good between us.'

Reaching up, she stroked his cheek. 'Do you promise?'

'Oh, yeah,' he said slowly.

And she believed him because she could see the certainty and love he was feeling reflected in his eyes as he lowered his mouth to kiss her again.

EPILOGUE

DESPITE THE WEATHER forecast predicting rain, the clouds emptied from the sky just as the limousine turned slowly into Broad Street. Glancing up at the sun, and then back down to the diamond ring on her third finger, Teddie smiled. She knew from personal experience that predicting the future was an extremely unreliable business.

'Do you like it?'

Looking up into Aristo's face, she nodded slowly. The ring was a surprise gift to mark six months of married life—*happily* married life—and it was stunning, but the soft grip of his hand around hers was what was making her heart swell with love.

Any fears she might have had of history repeating itself were long forgotten. Aristo had been true to his word and as eager as she to make sure that the mistakes of the past stayed in the past.

'Of course I do.' Reaching up, she stroked his cheek, her green eyes suddenly teasing.

'Do I get one every six months?'

He laughed, and then his face grew serious. 'I know it's not an official anniversary—it's just that I wanted to give you something...you know, because last time—'

'I know.' Leaning forward, she kissed him, cutting off his words.

Their engagement had lasted a year, and both of them had enjoyed the wait. They'd argued a little, and laughed a lot, and then finally they'd had a small private wedding with friends and colleagues that they'd planned together. Elliot had given Teddie away, and George had been a very solemn page boy, and now six months had passed and they had never felt closer.

'I love you,' she said softly.

Sliding his hand around her waist he pulled her closer. 'I love you too.' His eyes were steady and unblinking. 'And I know it's been a difficult lately, but that's going to end today.'

'It's fine. I understand.'

Today, after months and months of intense preparation, Aristo was finally floating his business on the New York Stock Exchange. He'd been working long hours, and she knew he was trying to reassure her now, but it was something she no longer needed.

The unhappy memories of their first marriage were just memories.

Now, instead of staying late at the office, he'd invite his team back to the apartment so that she and George could be a part of the process, and she wasn't left feeling isolated and lonely. And on the odd occasion when he had been forced to travel he had kept his trips as short as possible, often returning earlier than expected or taking her and George with him.

She squeezed his hand. 'And today's going to be better than fine.' Feeling the limo start to slow, she kissed him fiercely, her eyes burning with love. 'I'm so proud of you, Aristo.'

He shrugged. 'I work with some good people. They're really what's made this possible.'

'You do, and you've worked incredibly hard too.' Her gaze fixed on his face. 'But I wasn't talking about the business,' she said softly. 'I was talking about you.'

Aristo stared down into her clear green eyes, his heart pounding.

The limo had stopped. If he looked out of the window he would be able to see the six Corinthian columns of the New York Stock Exchange. For so long he had dreamed of this moment—the short walk to the legendary neoclassical building that would turn his business into a global brand.

But over the last eighteen months he'd made a far more important journey with the woman sitting beside him. Teddie had transformed his life. She had taught him how to hope, to believe and to love.

Of course he was pleased that the IPO was happening, but the appeal of the big deal had dimmed. His life with Teddie and George was far more satisfying and exciting than any boardroom negotiation, and he savoured every moment spent with his wife and son for he had come so close to losing them.

As soon as they stepped out onto the pavement time seemed to speed up exponentially, so that one moment the second bell of the day was ringing to start trading on the Leonidas stock and the next they were mingling with underwriters and executives from the business.

And now they were back in the limousine, on the way to a party for the staff at Leonidas headquarters.

Teddie breathed out slowly. After the frenzy of the trading floor the car seemed incredibly calm and quiet.

She felt Aristo's gaze on her face and, turning, she smiled up at him. 'Happy?' she said softly.

He nodded. 'It went well.' Leaning forward, he tapped on the glass behind the driver's head. 'Bob, can you take us to the apartment now, please?'

Teddie frowned. 'But what about the party? Don't you want to celebrate?'

He shook his head. 'I spoke to the staff this morning. They know how pleased I am, and this party will be a lot more fun for them without the boss breathing down their necks.'

Biting her lip, she touched her fingertips to his cheek. 'Does that mean I get to have you all to myself?'

Pulling her into his arms, he laughed.

'Yes.' He paused. 'And no. I thought we needed

some time as a family, so I've arranged for us to spend a week at the island. We're just going to pick up George on the way.' His eyes dropped to her mouth. 'But once we're there we should have time to celebrate...*privately.*'

The dark heat in his gaze took her breath away. 'I like the sound of that,' she said slowly. 'And we have got a lot to celebrate.'

More than she would ever have imagined, and more than Aristo knew.

Watching her expression shift, Aristo frowned. 'I'm happy it's all over, Teddie, but going public with the business isn't what I want to celebrate.'

His face was so serious, so open, that she could keep the secret to herself no longer.

'I wasn't just talking about the business.'

Leaning closer, she fixed her eyes on his handsome face, wanting to see his reaction. He looked at her uncertainly and, picking up his hand, she pressed it gently against her stomach.

'We're having a baby.'

For a moment he didn't speak—neither of them could: their emotions were too intense, too raw. But it didn't matter. She could see everything he was feeling in his heart, everything she needed to see burning in his eyes as he pulled her closer and kissed her passionately.

* * * * *